THE WATERCRESS FILE

Borgo Press Books by Victor J. Banis

THE WATERCRESS FILE

FILE

BEING THE FURTHER
ADVENTURES OF THAT
MAN FROM C.A.M.P.

VICTOR J. BANIS

THE BORGO PRESS
MMXII

THE WATERCRESS FILE

FIRST BORGO PRESS EDITION

Published by Wildside Press LLC

www.wildsidebooks.com

THE WATERCRESS FILE

CONTENTS

FOREWORD TO THE BORGO PRESS EDITION

The books in the series, *The Man from C.A.M.P.*, were among the earliest of the many novels I have penned. They were written in the 1960s, and they are very much a part of that exciting era when people of so many different sorts were coming out of so many different closets. Gay people were celebrating in the streets the very same lifestyle that only a few years before had engendered in many of us guilt and shame and fear, ruined large numbers of promising careers and sent many to prison.

These books were a part of my celebration. They were written with tongue very firmly in cheek, in a few days each, with nary a thought of rewrite or polishing up some admittedly amateurish prose. They were never intended to be "literature," and they are not. They were, however, intended to be fun.

I think they still are.

—Victor J. Banis

THE MAN FROM C.A.M.P. CHECKLIST

1. *The Man from C.A.M.P.*
2. **Color Him Gay*
3. **The WATERCRESS File*
4. *The Son Goes Down*
5. *Gothic Gaye*
6. *Holiday Gay*
7. *Rally Round the Fag*
8. **The Gay Dogs*
9. *Blow the Man Down*
10. *Gay-Safe* (not written by Victor Banis)

Associated Titles:

Sex and the Single Gay
*The C.A.M.P. Guide to Astrology
*The C.A.M.P. Cookbook

*=Published by Borgo Press

CHAPTER ONE

JACKIE HOLMES SIGHED dreamily and ran one hand fondly over the expanse of naked, ivory-colored skin next to him on the bed. The ivory skin stirred, and his companion's incredibly long eyelashes fluttered open. Lin's bewitchingly pretty face broke into a happy smile as he saw Jackie.

"Again?" Lin asked in the soft, musical voice that sent little darts of excited anticipation chasing one another up and down Jackie's spine.

Jackie beamed and nodded his head in quick agreement. "Again," he said, moving happily into the open arms. Lin embraced him gently at first, still lethargic with the clinging sleep from which he had been awakened. Jackie's hands, however, were busy on the silklike smoothness of the naked flesh, making their way down the curve of the spine, fondling the delicious softness of the mounds, exploring the warm moistness of delight between them. Lin was shedding the sleep rapidly, his body stirring as it woke, his arms clinging more tightly to Jackie.

"The flower of the backyard," Jackie whispered as his searching fingers reached the core of Lin's erogenous zone. Lin laughed softly at the remark. "You are familiar with Chin P'ing Mei," he asked.

"The Golden Lotus?" Jackie said, his fingers pleading silently for an invitation to what he suspected was an enchanted playground. "I've read it." *The Golden Lotus* of which they spoke was one of the most notorious, and most stimulating, works of oriental erotica. The term that Jackie had used was one that came from the work, one used in connection with backward loving.

"Then you'll understand," Lin went on. "If I say that the blossom waits to be plucked."

Jackie understood, all right, and he didn't need a second invitation. He allowed Lin to turn, dropping to the floor and kneeling to rest his upper body upon the bed, his skin exposed and raised. Jackie admired it hungrily—the golden half moons, and nestled between them, the blossom of which they had spoken, a mere dot that looked inadequate for the size of Jackie's ready excitement.

"You're too small," Jackie said regretfully, leaning across Lin's bent body in frustration. "It'll hurt you too much."

Lin chuckled softly and wriggled an invitation. "The tiniest of buds may unfold to reveal an ample rose," he argued. "But knock at the door, and it will open to you."

Jackie gladly gave up the argument, nor did he resist when Lin, impatient, reached for him and guided him to the target. He was right—the door did open to him, and there was room enough, even completely. If Lin suffered any pain, he disguised the fact well. He moaned softly with pleasure as he was thrilled to the brim, and reached behind to squeeze Jackie's buttocks, pulling Jackie even closer.

"There isn't any more," Jackie told him with a laugh. "Unless you want my arm too."

For an answer, Lin only quivered and began to twist maddeningly, pushing the springy softness of his buttocks back against Jackie. Jackie began to move too, slowly at first and then faster and faster as the enchanted chamber began to work its magic. It was pretty potent magic and, to Jackie's regret, the end came all too quickly. Surprisingly, at the first convulsive spasm within himself that signaled Jackie's finish, Lin too erupted in a burning, torrential finish, that left them both limp and exhausted.

Afterward, Jackie held Lin happily in his arms, talking little and kissing a great deal. The morning sun, filtering through the closed draperies, told him it must be nearly noon, but he was in no hurry to get up. In fact, it was just beginning to look as though they were ready for still another round when the phone rang.

He frowned in annoyance, the hand that had been feeling around at Lin's legs pausing. It would be easy to ignore the jangling bell, and take advantage of the growing tenseness in his hand.

The telephone seemed to be louder and more insistent with each ring. Jackie sighed and let go of Lin to reach for the receiver.

"Jackie?" It was a woman's voice, high pitched and rather tremulous. Jackie recognized it at once.

"Aunt Lily," he said, pleased to hear her voice despite the fun she had interrupted. "I haven't heard from you in ages. Where are you?"

"Oh, I'm at home," she explained. "In Washington. But I was wondering—is there any likelihood that you'll be coming by this way?"

It seemed to Jackie rather a nonsensical question. He was in Los Angeles, where he ordinarily lived, and Aunt Lily was all the way across the country, in Washington, D.C.

"I hadn't planned on seeing you today," he answered. "Why, is there anything the matter?"

"I don't know," she said in a sober tone of voice. "I could be mistaken, but I somehow think we've stumbled upon something. It seems to be a message of some sort...."

"A message?" Jackie's attention quickened. "What sort of message?"

"I don't know, exactly," she admitted. "It's in some sort of code. But there is a little drawing at the bottom, almost as if it might be a signature."

"Can you describe the drawing?"

"Oh, quite easily. It's plainly a butterfly."

Jackie caught his breath sharply—a coded message, signed with a butterfly. Aunt Lily was right—unless he was very mistaken, she had indeed stumbled upon something—maybe something extremely big.

"It's a long story," she was saying.

"Save it until I get there," Jackie said quickly, interrupted her. "I should be there sometime this evening, if I can get a reservation."

"Oh, how wonderful. I'll have tea ready," Aunt Lily gushed.

Lin was sitting up by the time Jackie finished the conversation, looking rather disappointed. "You will have to go out?" he asked.

"Way out," Jackie agreed. "All the way to Washington, D.C."

"Too bad," Lin said, looking at his still aroused condition. "And just when things were getting interesting."

Jackie smiled and leaned over to plant a kiss briefly on the center of Lin's interest. "Save me the leftovers, and I'll warm them up when I get back."

Lin giggled, and got up out of the bed, dressing with

natural grace. Jackie watched the appetizing frame being tucked into a pair of white pants, sighing as the golden flesh disappeared. Forcing his eyes away, he began to dress himself.

He waited until he had seen Lin out of the apartment, with a last, lingering kiss, and a promise to call as soon as he was back in town. He was grateful for the fact that Lin had not questioned him regarding the call or the nature of his trip to Washington—Jackie would have been unable to give him the honest answer.

Alone in the apartment, Jackie went to the phone and dialed two digits, waiting impatiently until a deep, masculine voice answered with a quick "Yes?"

"Rich, I've got to go on a little trip," Jackie explained hurriedly. "I'm leaving now for the airport—call ahead and get me a reservation on the next Washington flight. And call Ted Summers for me, tell him I'm on my way to Washington and he's to try to meet me at the airport. I'll leave word."

"Something big?" Rich asked on the other end.

"Looks like it might be," Jackie answered. "Big enough, at least, that I want to look into it myself. But I have a feeling I'll need some government help, and Summers is the only agent in Washington that I'm personally acquainted with. If nothing else, he'll know who I should talk to about it."

"Any message for him," Rick asked.

"Tell him it concerns Butterfly," Jackie said quickly. Without waiting for Rich to register surprise, Jackie hung up and hurried to the bedroom, quickly packing for the trip.

CHAPTER TWO

Of all the cities in the United States, Jackie thought, pressing his nose against the glass to look out the window, none could be more beautiful to see from the air, at night, than Washington. The pilot had come in low, banking slightly to allow the passengers a full, breathtaking view. The Washington Monument reached up into the sky, looking almost as if it would scrape the underside of the plane. Other monuments, each lighted artfully, were set like jewels in the tapestry of the city. And every where were the lights and color of Washington by night—the streets radiating out from the center, like the spokes of a wheel, creating a brilliant starburst effect.

The stewardess passed, pausing to indicate Jackie's still unfastened safety belt. He clasped it over his middle and watched as the ground loomed nearer. The landing gear had already descended with a loud thunk and a few minutes later the plane bounced slightly as it came down, touched the ground, and they were braking mightily as they swept down the runway.

As he entered the terminal, Jackie glanced around for Ted Summers, in case he'd beat him there by the special jet. There was no sight of him, and he was about to move on, expecting to find Summers at the baggage area, when a stranger stepped unexpectedly in front of him.

"Mr. Holmes," the stranger asked, his manner business-like and formal.

"Yes," Jackie answered, motionless but alert.

"Craig Mathews," the man said, flicking open his wallet to reveal his identification. "Of the C.I.A.— Summers couldn't make it, and he thought this might be more down our line anyway."

"I see," Jackie answered simply. In a sense, he was disappointed. He had looked forward to an encore with the handsome, masculine Treasury agent with whom he had worked before and who he had managed to bed before their partnership was ended.

On the other hand, he could hardly resent Craig Mathews as a replacement. The C.I.A. agent looked more like an ivy-league student—nut brown hair combed with extreme care in a continental style, a small but apparently well-formed body fitted into a four button suit and tab-collared shirt, with a finger thin tie. Rather a nice piece of homo-work, Jackie decided, something he really wouldn't mind boning up on.

His survey of Craig Mathews surface charms had

taken no more than a second. Now, smiling, he shook Craig's hand warmly in his own, and started down the hallway, with the agent falling into step beside him.

"New England?" he asked as they walked. He had noted a distinct accent in Craig's voice.

"Boston," Craig answered, without embellishment.

He was not, Jackie observed, bubbling over with good cheer.

"I'll have to get my bag," Jackie said as they neared the baggage pick up area.

"I'll have it picked up for you," Craig Mathews told him, steering him instead toward the exit. Jackie did not like the abrupt, nearly rude way in which he was being handled, but he did not for the moment offer any objections. He remained silent as he followed his companion outside.

As if by magic, a cab appeared in front of them. It was not, Jackie observed, in line with the others that took turns with the fares from the airport, but rather had been parked quite by itself. Efficient, he thought admiringly—in the cab, with another agent driving them, they could talk safely without fear of being overhead by the wrong party. Craig Mathews, Jackie noted, glanced carefully inside as he stooped to enter the cab. He was taking no chances on mistakes.

The cab had begun to move again almost before Jackie was inside. Jackie pulled the door closed and relaxed against the seat. The windows were closed, shutting out the bouyant April air, but he suspected that was deliberate, and did not try to open one.

"Now then," Mathews said finally. "What's this about Butterfly?"

"I wish I could tell you," Jackie answered with a grin. "But I don't know much myself. For all I can say, it might be just a wild goose chase."

Carefully and rapidly he explained about the call from Aunt Lily. "It might be nothing," he repeated. "But with a name as important as Butterfly, I didn't think it would do to take any chances."

"You're probably right," Mathews agreed, although he was frowning. No doubt, Jackie thought, watching the youthfully handsome agent, he was disappointed. And also uncomfortable—with some reason. If he knew about Jackie, presumably from Summers, he knew Jackie was gay—and made a policy of always getting his man.

"Did you get the address?" Mathews asked of the driver, leaning forward. The driver repeated Aunt Lily's address correctly. They were already driving in that direction.

They rode for a few blocks in silence. Jackie found himself wishing that his companion would thaw out slightly. Even if he didn't make the scene with Mathews, it was a shame to see anyone so attractive being so unfriendly.

"You know," Jackie said aloud finally, determined to break the ice. "I don't think you like me."

Mathews did not even look in his direction, nor did the expressionless mask on his face slip at all. "My instructions had nothing to say about liking you," he said simply.

Jackie winced—it wasn't a very good beginning, "I suppose you hate faggots," he said, allowing himself to be a little sarcastic.

Mathews shrugged. "Not particularly. I just prefer to be around my own type, as I'm sure you do as well."

"On the contrary, I like being around straight men," Jackie said. "Particularly the Irish type." With a big smile, he leaned toward the agent and clapped a hand loudly and brazenly on one of Mathew's legs, halfway between the knee and his nicely rounded crotch.

Mathews jumped as though he had been stuck with a pin. "Cool it," he snapped angrily, knocking Jackie's hand off his leg.

Jackie shrugged and folded his hands across his own lap. At least he had broken through that icy facade, which was an accomplishment. In the rear-view mirror, he saw the driver of the car watching the back seat, barely able to suppress his amusement. Jackie winked, and the driver started to chuckle. At the same time, he caught sight of Mathew's angry face, and swallowed the laugh, choking loudly instead.

Jackie did not attempt anything more in the way of ice-breakers. Better not push his luck too far, he decided, at least not right away. If by chance they were together for a while...well, that might be a different matter. There was no denying that Mathews was attractive. His complexion was inclined to be ruddy, although a faint shadow of freckles could be seen at the bridge of his nose. Beneath thick eyebrows, his wide eyes were a bright Kelly green. His nose, just avoiding being too large, tilted upward at the tip, and his mouth was a sharply etched and wide design above an angular chin. Boyish, handsome, and Irish as County Cork—except for the Mathews name. He made a mental note to ask about that later.

As for Craig's resentment—well, it was not hard to understand. Jackie had encountered it often enough, as did most homosexuals. Of course, he could have saved himself a certain degree of embarrassment by acting more masculine and less noticeably homosexual. But his effeminate mannerisms were essential, a mask that he wore in public as a part of his job.

Like Mathews, Jackie too was an agent, although not for the United States or any other government. His organization was international, and underground, a highly efficient network of agencies and people, dedicated to a common cause—the protection and advancement of homosexuals. It was called C.A.M.P., and there were few who knew of its existence, although many benefited from its work. Throughout the world, agents of different sections within the organization worked tirelessly—some of them attempting to improve the lot of the homosexual politically, some socially; some worked with medicine and others with the mind.

Jackie's field was protection, the super police activities necessary to protect and save homosexuals from the dangers of blackmail and violence. He had come to the field young, after an unfortunate experience, and he was one of C.A.M.P.'s top men. Although he appeared to be only an effeminate and probably helpless faggot, small, blond, and comfortably pretty, he was in fact a man of awesome feats and capabilities. His aim with a gun was so perfect that neither he nor anyone else could remember a single shot within the last five years that had not hit its intended target. Although he was slender, he was not at all weak. With a wiry strength that belied his size, and a full understanding of nearly all the arts of self-defense, from judo to karate, from wrestling to sword fighting, he was a match for any adversary.

Craig Mathews, however, could not know any of this, for his files would have little to say about C.A.M.P., and less about Jackie Holmes. Mathews would know only that Jackie was a homosexual, working for a homosexual outfit, and that Ted Summers, the T-man who knew Jackie, had passed on a message and warned that Jackie's suggestions were not to be taken lightly.

Staring out the window on his own side of the car, Mathews was thinking exactly those thoughts. He did not like the assignment at all, nor his companion. Summers had indicated that Holmes was a sharp individual, but Mathews could see little to admire about the nelly queen sitting next to him. Chances were, fortunately, that there would be little to the assignment.

It was not likely that some zany relative of this fairy's had actually stumbled upon anything connected with Butterfly, the super-secret, world-wide spy organization that was a source of fear to most of the world governments.

The top agents of two dozen nations, to say nothing of the U.N. and Interpol, were rarely able to come up with any information as to their activities—so although he could not afford to pass up the lead, Mathews had little hope for the outcome. In the meantime, he hoped to hell that the blond faggot next to him would just keep his hands to himself.

CHAPTER THREE

IF CRAIG MATHEWS WAS unenthusiastic about Jackie's presence, he was totally unprepared for the creature who greeted them at the door of the house to which they had gone. Gladiola had the large bones, the sculptured features and the ebony skin that make many Negro women ravishing.

Gladiola was not ravishing, however. For one thing, she was past the "ravishing" age. For another, there was just too much of her. She was immense of figure, and unlike some large women, who carry themselves with such grace of movement that one is hardly aware of their size, Gladiola seemed determined to make herself look even bigger with her brightly printed dress—a mass of oversize flowers of every imaginable hue, against a white background.

"Mr. Jackie," she cried loudly, grinning broadly. "How wonderful to see you." The word came out sounding like wunnraful, and it was Jackie's guess that Gladiola was more than a little intoxicated, not an unusual condition for her.

He knew her well enough, however, to know that her drinking was essentially harmless, and a vice ordinarily overlooked by the family, in favor of her virtues. She had been with the family more years than she would allow anyone to mention, and when at one time the finances of the family had slipped so that Aunt Lily had been unable to pay her wages, Gladiola had not only stayed on, but pitched in with her savings to help out until things had gotten better. She was as kind and generous as she was fat, which was saying a great deal.

"Hello, Gladiola," Jackie greeted her warmly, allowing her to hug him with all the tenderness of an angry grizzly. One whiff of her breath was enough to confirm his suspicions about her condition. "This is Mr. Mathews, of the government. He's come with me to see Aunt Lily."

"Oh, she's practically birthing babies over your visit," Gladiola informed him. She shook hands with Craig Mathews, leaving him shaking his pained fingers afterward and glancing at them in search of bone damage as Gladiola led them down the hall to the parlor.

"She's in the kitchen," Gladiola said, ushering them into the parlor. "I'll go tell her you're here."

"I'll come along," Jackie said, starting after her. "Make yourself at home, Mr. Mathews, we'll be right back."

Left alone, Craig Mathews could only stand and puzzle over the odd situation. From the moment he had entered the house, it was as though he had stepped back in time, to the turn of the century. The house was a study in antiquity, the rooms musty with faded velvet and tarnished gilt.

He scowled and cocked his head to one side, listening. Had he only imagined it, or had he heard a whispered "psst?"

There it was again, and decidedly not imagined. Puzzled, he turned, his eyes widening as he did so. He had not heard the elderly woman enter the room from the other door, although he was sure she had not been there when he came in. Nor was he any more prepared for her than he had been for Gladiola. In appearance, this one was more conventional. In a photograph, she would have appeared as the model for someone's grandmother—gray haired and blatantly aging, a short, plumpish little creature who was to be imagined knitting and rocking, with a contented smile on her face.

She was not, however, knitting and rocking now. She was leaning against the door frame in what, so far as he could judge, was intended as a seductive pose, although it fell far short of that goal. Her over-long skirt had been hiked up to reveal one bony, misshapen knee. One rheumatic hip was thrust out, a hand upon it. The top three buttons of her high-collared dress had been undone, and the dress pulled over one shoulder, a la a movie siren. All in all, the sight was both ludicrous and appalling.

As he stared at her in amazement, she winked lecherously and clicked her tongue. "Hello, handsome," she greeted him with a cracked voice. "How's about you and me having a little romp before the others get here."

"I beg your pardon?" Mathews could scarcely believe he had heard her correctly. This sweet-looking old lady could not really be propositioning him.

"You know," she told him with a leer, wriggling the knee. "Tear off a little joy."

Mathews swallowed and shook his head numbly. "I don't think that's a good idea."

"What's a matter?" she asked, eyes narrowed suspiciously. "You got no guts?"

"Aunt Nasturtia," A voice behind him said sharply. "Don't scare him off."

Mathews jumped and whirled about again, slightly relieved to see someone who looked at least normal. In fact, the buxom blonde before him was not bad, although a little vulgar and earthy for his taste. Her ample breasts were all but spilling out of her barely fastened blouse, and her skirt was sufficiently skin tight to conceal little of her figure.

"Don't mind Aunt Nasturtia," the blonde was saying in an unpleasant, nasal voice. "To tell the truth, she's a nympho."

Aunt Nasturtia gave a disgruntled snort and hobbled past Mathews and out of the room, fixing a cold stare briefly on the blonde's head before she disappeared out of sight.

"I'm Mari," the blonde informed Craig with a wink of her own. "That's short for Marigold."

Craig frowned thoughtfully, ignoring the blunt hint in her smile—Aunt Nasturtia was not the only nympho in the house, if he was any judge. "Lily, Nasturtia, Marigold—is everybody in the house named like a flower?"

"Um-hum, ain't it a gas?" Her smile faded as the strains of "The Minute Waltz" sounded from nearby. For the first few measures, the notes were perfect. The beauty of the music was marred, however, by a clinker of a note. The pianist stopped, and then started over at the beginning. Craig smiled as the same note was again struck wrong, and the music paused once more. This time the pianist began the first movement of the "Moonlight Sonata" instead.

At that moment, Jackie returned, with yet another elderly figure. This one seemed at least more sane than the other, a tall, willowy creature with quick, intelligent eyes and animated gestures.

"Mr. Mathews, this is my Aunt Lily," Jackie said. Mathews took the offered hand, surprised by the hearty squeeze he received.

"Jackie says I'm to tell you all about our experience," Aunt Lily said with a nervous smile.

"I think that might be a good idea," Mathews agreed. He was beginning to feel that the sooner he got out of this place, the better he would be. They were obviously looney; for all he knew, they might be dangerous. That one old girl had looked positively capable of devouring him—for that matter, Holmes appeared capable of that, in a manner of speaking.

* * * * * * *

"Now then," Craig said when they had seated themselves. "Suppose you explain about Butterfly. As I understand it, you've stumbled upon some sort of message, is that right?"

"Well, I think so," Aunt Lily agreed. "But it's in a code apparently, so I don't really know what kind of message, or if it even is a message. I'd better start at the beginning."

Craig nodded his approval.

"Well," she began. "It started this morning. You see, we have a poodle—Fritzie. Do you know Jackie's poodle, Sophie?"

Mathews had to admit that he had not, ignoring Jackie's quick smile of amusement. "They're twins," Aunt Lily went on. "Except for the sex, of course. But the thing is, they're both white, and rather spoiled, I'm afraid."

Mathews was having a difficult time seeing how all this tied in with Butterfly, nor was he particularly interested in their choice of pets.

"And it was raining, this morning," Aunt Lily said emphatically, as though that explained everything, which of course it did not.

"I see," Craig said helplessly.

"Oh, dear, I don't think I'm explaining this very well," Aunt Lily said, putting a hand to her face.

Mathews was about to agree with her, but Jackie spoke before he had the opportunity. "Take your time," he said, "And don't worry, Mr. Mathews is very patient."

"Of course," Mathews agreed without enthusiasm.

"Well, it was the rain. Nasturtia didn't know it was raining, you see—have you met Nasturtia, Mr. Mathews? I can call her...."

"I've had the pleasure," Mathews informed her hurriedly. He had no immediate desire to further confuse the conversation by including the other aunt in it.

"Anyway, it was raining, and Nasturtia didn't notice, and she let Fritzie out into the yard to play. Well, you can imagine what Fritzie looked like when he came back in, just covered with mud and all. So I told Nasturtia she'd have to take him to the beauty parlor, only our regular shop was booked up, and couldn't take him, so Nasturtia went to another one just down the street, one we had never been to before."

Mathews nodded, although he still was not able to discern the point of the story, and wondered if she might have forgotten why he was here.

"They did a lovely job on him, I must admit," Lily went on. "Except that when Nasturtia went back to pick him up, they had put clips on his ears—little sequined butterflies."

Mathews attempted to conceal his disappointment— was this all she had been talking about?—a pair of costume pins for a dog?

Jackie too had a twinge of disappointment, but he knew Aunt Lily well enough to recognize at once that she had more to say. At that moment, however, Nasturtia, who must have been listening in the hall, appeared in the doorway.

"It isn't my fault," she snapped defensively, although she had not in fact been accused of anything. "I told them not to put anything like that on Fritz—he's a boy, after all."

"But they did put the pins on, and you didn't even notice," Aunt Lily said in a tone that indicated this subject had already been discussed at length between the two of them.

"Well, I had things on my mind," Nasturtia grumbled in a weaker voice.

Mari, who had been quiet up to this point, snorted disdainfully. "You may as well admit it," she said. To Aunt Lily, she explained, "She told me that the clipper there was a doll, and she was all excited over him. That's why she couldn't think of anything else."

"Mari," Aunt Lily said reproachfully.

"Well you needn't sound so smug," Aunt Nasturtia said petulantly to Mari. "Just suppose you tell how you went to the store with five dollars in your purse, bought all those things for Lily, and came back with five."

Aunt Lily raised one eyebrow quizzically and turned to Mari, silently indicating she would like an explanation.

Mari glowered at Nasturtia for a moment before dropping her eyes to the floor. "Well," she mumbled. "I met this sailor on the bus...."

"On the bus!" Lily was shocked.

"It was practically empty," Mari said quickly, with a brief smile. "And we were all the way in the back. Anyway, he put his jacket over us, so nobody could see anything if they looked."

Nasturtia giggled triumphantly, and Lily only frowned her disapproval silently. Jackie coughed to hide his amusement, which was heightened by the crimson blush that flashed over Mathews face. The agent was finding the family a little hard to believe.

"I think you'd better go on and finish your story," Jackie said, heading off any possible quarrel. He was eager to hear the further details anyway.

"Of course," Lily agreed, giving both the other two ladies withering glances before she smiled in Mr. Mathews direction. "When Nasturtia brought Fritz in, with those awful little pins on his ears, I'm afraid I was a little perturbed. I scolded her, and then I took the pins off, but I was annoyed and I wasn't too careful. One of them broke, and to my surprise, there was this note hidden inside it."

"I wouldn't have read it," Nasturtia said cheerfully, "But I thought it was a love note from the clipper."

Lily glowered coldly at her again, before producing a crumpled scrap of paper from her pocket. "To tell the truth, I wasn't immediately suspicious," she explained. "But then I saw it was in a code of some sort. That, and the fact that it was hidden, made me wonder. And then, there was the fact that it was a mistake—I mean, our getting the note."

"A mistake?" Mathews asked. He was watching the note eagerly, plainly impatient to see it. Aunt Lily, however, was intent on finishing her explanation before she handed over the note.

"Well, it seems there was another woman there when Nasturtia went to pick up Fritz. And she was picking up a white poodle also. I think they put the clips on the wrong dog, since Nasturtia had instructed them to put nothing on Fritz, and the other dog was bare."

"Sounds logical," Mathews agreed. He managed a slight grin as Lily at last relinquished the note, handing it over to him.

Even from where he sat, Jackie saw the rough sketch at the bottom, the drawing of a butterfly that served, as Aunt Lily had guessed, as a signature. There was no mistake about that, it was a symbol that was known to agents and spies about the world, the sign of the most notorious and dangerous underground organization in existence—Butterfly.

Mathews recognized it too, and his expression went from surprise to grim appraisal, to suppressed excitement.

"It looks authentic, all right," he admitted, still studying the note. "I'd stake my reputation on it."

Jackie had risen to look over his shoulder at the note. "So would I," he said. Mathews gave him a frosty look. "If I had one, I mean," Jackie amended

Mathews ignored that remark, folding the note and placing it carefully inside his billfold. "If you don't mind, I'll take care of it from here in," he said to Aunt Lily. His manner toward her had become less skeptical, since he had seen the note.

"But what does it say?" she asked. "Heavens, I think

we're entitled to know that."

"I wish I knew," he said with a shake of his head. "Unfortunately, it's a code I haven't seen yet. But don't worry, our boys will break it in no time flat."

He rose to go, the others standing also. As they did so, Mathews became aware again of the "Moonlight Sonata." It first movement was just ending, but he was certain that the same movement had already ended earlier. What's more, he had originally thought it was the batty one, Nasturtia, who had been playing, but she was with them now. "Who's playing?" he asked politely.

"That's Honey," Aunt Nasturtia answered proudly.

"Entertaining a boy friend," Mari added, in a none too pleasant voice.

"Now, dear," Lily scolded her mildly. "Don't be envious. There's nothing to prevent you from meeting your own men-friends, and bringing them home."

"I wouldn't dare," Mari said, rolling her eyes. "I did once, and between Honey and Aunt Nasturtia, the poor thing was worn out before I could even get to him myself."

Mathews paled slightly at the prospect of still another nymphomaniac in the house. It was beginning to seem to him that he might not be at all safe here—these women were too hungry for male flesh, and they were not the sort to whom he customarily offered his male flesh.

"Why is Honey playing the first movement over and over?" he asked, however, curious about that fact, for the first movement had indeed begun for the third time.

"The dear thing only knows the first movement," Lily explained. "But wait, Honey will want to meet you."

Before Mathews could protest. Lily had floated away in search of the pianist. The music stopped a moment later. Mathews shifted his weight nervously from one foot to the other, and waited, prepared to bolt for the front door if necessary.

It was not, as he expected, a woman who returned with Aunt Lily, but a man—or an approximation of one, he corrected himself. In comparison to this one, Holmes was as masculine as a Marine commando.

"Hi, I'm Honey," the young man greeted him with an overly warm smile. His eyes went up and down Craig's body, and Craig felt a warning draft as his clothes were metaphorically stripped from him.

"Isn't that rather an odd name?" Mathews asked faintly.

Honey nodded his head. "It's short for Honeysuckle," he explained. "We all have floral names, if you hadn't noticed."

"Why not Pansy?" Craig could not resist asking. "That's a flower too."

Far from being annoyed, Honey only chuckled. Watching him, Jackie was not so perturbed as Mathews. In fact, he was far from it. It was true, Honey was effeminate, the type often described as languid.

He had grown, however, since Jackie had last seen him, into a terribly pretty queen—thin, but with a graceful elegance about his appearance and movements. His trousers were rather loose fitting, but even so Jackie had seen a nicely formed, if small, fanny, and now that Honey was facing him, he could scarcely ignore the outline in the trousers that, unless his eyes were playing tricks on him, extended nearly halfway to the knees—and Honey had very long legs! Nelly or not, Honey had quite a lot to offer—and Jackie found himself looking forward to the offer.

That, however, would have to be later. He forced his eyes from Honey's leg, meeting Honey's understanding smile with a wink. Business first, before Honey's business.

"I'll tag along with you," he said to Mathews. "I'm curious about that note myself."

"It isn't necessary," Mathews told him. He was beginning to feel dazed by the strange people who inhabited this house, and had no desire to keep company with any of them longer than necessary.

"I'd like to, though," Jackie insisted. "After all, I flew all the way here from the West Coast just to see if that was authentic. I'm entitled to be a little curious now."

Mathews yielded, more interested in reaching the safety outside than in arguing. "Well, all right," he agreed, heading for the door. "But we'd better get with it."

Jackie followed him, pausing at the door to look back at the others. "I'll be back later," he promised. "That is, if you can find room for me. I could always sleep on a sofa."

"Or you could double up with Honey," Nasturtia said.

Honey grinned. "Sounds fine," he said, his voice a purr. "Those sofas are beastly anyway."

CHAPTER FOUR

MATHEWS' "TAXI" WAS STILL waiting outside, the driver looking as patient and fresh as though he had been there only a minute or two. "My place," Craig instructed him as they climbed in. Jackie followed him inside and sat back in silence.

"I gather the family was quite a surprise to you," Jackie said finally.

Now that he was safely away from them, Craig could afford to grin slightly. "I'll have to admit, they are different," he said in a voice that might have been genuinely amused, or sarcastic, for all Jackie could tell. Mathews' mask was an all-time thing, and thus far just about impenetrable.

"Speaking of families, reminds me," Jackie said, deciding to try another approach. "How did a no-mystery-about-it Irishman like you ever get a name like Mathews? Wouldn't O'Malley have been more appropriate?"

For the first time the mask seemed really to slip, and when he spoke, Mathews might have been talking to a friend instead of a casual business acquaintance whom he was keeping at arm's length.

"Would ye laugh?" he asked in a brogue so thick it could have been cut with a knife. "If I tell you it should have been O'Malley?"

"I won't laugh at all," Jackie answered with sincerity. "But I'll admit you've got me curious."

"It's not that much of a story," Craig said, in his normal voice. "My mother was first generation, and still pure Irish. She'd have no part of any young man who wasn't from the Isles, although there was one who was daft about her—Mathews, his name was."

"I'd guess he finally changed her mind," Jackie said with a smile.

"He did that—but not until after I had come on the scene—oh, not fully, mind. I wasn't yet a baby boy, but I was more than a twinkle in my father's eye. He was a fine handsome devil, so my mother told me when she finally confessed the story. He wooed her and won her, but he wouldn't wed."

"An age old story," Jackie said.

"Yes. So, her father, of course, was all for taking a horsewhip to him and making him marry, but you know the pride of the Irish, and once he'd laughed at her, me mother wouldn't have him. So while I was making my presence felt, and seen, she remained a single girl, and Mr. Mathews continued to court her.

Finally she told him about me, and about her folly, and he just laughed and said he'd known about that since the morning after, and it made not an ort of difference. So they were married a month before I joined the family, and instead of the Timothy O'Malley I was to have been, I was Craig Mathews."

He paused and sat quietly for a moment, and Jackie thought he was perhaps embarrassed to have talked so much, to someone he hardly knew, and little liked.

"So now you know," Craig said at length, "that you're with the worst sort of companion a man could ask for—an illegitimate Irish Catholic, from Boston."

Jackie's first impulse was to laugh, but he realized in the nick of time that he was being dared to laugh—Craig was quite serious, summing up any complaints and asking to be reassured.

"As a matter of fact, I'd be hard pressed to think of a better companion," Jackie said instead. "It's not every day I get to ride around with a heavenly youth from the Emerald Isles, full of stuff and blarney."

Even the driver had to laugh at that, and Craig joined in, although he blushed also as he remembered that the young man with him was an admitted and obviously active homosexual.

They arrived then at their destination, what at first glance appeared to be merely a cleaning plant. As Jackie followed Craig inside, he realized that was only a front. Inside, behind a curtained dressing room, another door let them into a small but efficient-looking office.

"I just want to copy this," Craig explained, removing the note. "I'll send it to headquarters for decoding, with our driver. But I want to make a copy for us, in case anything should happen to him."

"Make two copies," Jackie suggested. "In case anything happens to you."

Craig shot him a quick glance, but he did not argue, and when he returned from the adjoining room a moment later, he had two copies, one of which he handed to Jackie, the other he locked in a drawer.

"I'll be right back," he said as he went back to the front of the shop. "I want to give Fred the original and send him on his way."

He was back again in a minute. "Now we wait," he announced. "How about some coffee?"

"No thanks," Jackie answered, seating himself on a small, Naugahyde-covered divan and loosening his necktie. He rarely needed stimulants of any sort; he was trained to be always alert and ready at any time.

"Sorry I can't offer anything to help pass the time," Craig said, sitting at the desk.

"I could make suggestions," Jackie said with a meaningful smile. "But I doubt you'd appreciate them, let alone go along with them."

"You're right," Craig agreed quickly, keeping his face expressionless.

Very frustrating, Jackie decided with a frown. He wondered if that one even showed any feeling when he was reaching a magnificent explosion. Of course, he'd like nothing better than an opportunity to answer that question through firsthand experience. But thus far he wasn't making much progress toward creating that opportunity.

Oh well, there was always Honey back at the house. He was grateful for the fact that he was versatile. He had always made it a policy to be what the other one wasn't. He found that he enjoyed many more opportunities that way.

"Of course," he said aloud, changing the subject. "We could just go to this poodle parlor and see what we can find."

"It would be closed by this time of night," Mathews reminded him. "And we can hardly break in without some more conclusive evidence. And we won't have that until we know what the note says."

So they waited. And an hour and a half later, they were still waiting. By the time the phone on Craig's desk rang, the agent was so nervous that he nearly hit the ceiling. Jackie, too, was impatient, although he was less nervous. He had been trained to remain calm in any situation, in order to function more efficiently.

Mathews could not hide his disappointment, however, as he listened to the speaker on the other end of the line, speaking only an occasional monosyllable himself. His face was grim as he finally hung up the phone and turned to Jackie.

"We're out of luck. The boys haven't been able to break that code yet. They think it might be unbreakable."

"Would you object if I took this along with me?" Jackie asked, indicating his copy of the note.

"What for?" Mathews asked.

"C.A.M.P., the organization I work for, has as fine a staff of code experts as exists anywhere in the world. I won't believe this thing is really unbreakable until they have had a crack at it."

Mathews was rather disdainful. "If our boys couldn't do anything with it, I hardly think it likely that your amateurs would do better."

"It can't hurt anything to let them try." Jackie pointed out. "We're not doing anything but sitting here wasting time anyway."

Mathews shrugged carelessly. "I suppose you're right there. But where do we find your people without going all the way to Los Angeles?"

"Oh, Los Angeles is only a local office, just as the one here in Washington is. Each of them operates more or less independently, but always under the assistance of High Camp, or headquarters."

"And where is...your headquarters?"

"Even I don't know that," Jackie admitted. "It could be anywhere on this earth, or maybe even off of it."

"Doesn't that make your work a little more difficult?" Craig asked.

"Not really. We're in constant communication—not directly, but through the local offices. And think of it this way, isn't it a lot safer if no one knows where to find you? Look how many risks would be eliminated if no one knew where our government was located, or our atomic defenses."

"I guess you're right," Mathews admitted begrudgingly; it annoyed him for some peculiar reason to think that this fairy might be able to say something intelligent. Everyone knew gay fellows were giddy and silly, and incapable of thinking deeply.

"Then I can take this message to C.A.M.P., and let the local office have a look at it?"

"All right, but on one condition," Craig agreed. "I'll go along, just to be sure there isn't anything out of the way."

"Fine," Jackie said, with a sly grin. "But you may find things a bit unorthodox."

"That I don't doubt," Mathews said, remembering Jackie's peculiar relatives—and Jackie himself was unique, so far as that went.

They left the office and Mathews led the way to a parking lot in the rear, where a Volkswagon was parked. "Since our chauffeur never came back, we'll have to go on our own steam," he said, climbing behind the wheel. "Where to?"

"Lafayette Park," Jackie instructed him.

Mathews gave him a funny glance. The park, although it was directly across the street from the nation's most famous residence, the White House, was also notorious as a pick-up spot for homosexuals. With the traffic inside and outside the park, it was a pretty unlikely place to conduct any sort of business, particularly that of an agent.

"You're sure," he asked aloud.

"Much surer than I am about you," Jackie said.

Mathews frowned and started off in the direction of the park. He had been warned that this would be unorthodox, and it had been his idea to come along—although he was beginning to regret that idea a little.

The park, as Craig had suspected, was a busy place. Young men in conspicuously tight jeans ambled up and down the walks, eyeing one another for a glimmer of interest; Mathews felt as though he were a lamb tossed into a den of hungry lions, although it was obvious that his companion was enjoying himself.

"Stop glowering and look flirtatious," Jackie whispered as they walked. "You're supposed to look like you belong here."

"I can't do that," Craig argued.

"Fake it—pretend one of them is Ava Gardner, and another one Lana Turner."

Craig did as suggested, with a slight improvement, but his heart wasn't really in the act. He was just plain uncomfortable, and out of place. He had no idea why they were here, or what was coming next.

The area of the park in which they were now was dark and secluded, and for a brief moment there was no one else around. With a movement so quick that Craig scarcely realized what was happening, Jackie had left the path and ducked behind a tree, waving for Craig to follow him.

By the time Craig was there, Jackie had already tripped a switch concealed somewhere on the tree, that caused a trap door to open suddenly in the ground. So cleverly was it placed that, from even a few inches away, the opening was hidden by the bushes and the tree.

"Come on," Jackie urged as Mathews stared in amazement. Mathews recovered sufficiently to follow Jackie down the steps that the opening had revealed. As they descended, the opening closed over their heads, and they were in darkness.

CHAPTER FIVE

THE DARKNESS LASTED FOR only a moment. Mathews was temporarily blinded by the brilliant light that caught him full in the face. Not until the light had dimmed did he realize that they were being examined.

"The password?" A voice from out of nowhere asked.

Jackie was silent for a moment, and Craig began to fear the blond agent might have forgotten the password. He experienced a dismal vision of the two of them waiting for days in the darkness of this pit. Finally, to his relief, Jackie answered, "Rim queen."

The light disappeared, and a second later a door opened in front of them, revealing a short, more comfortably-lighted hall. Jackie led the way down it, the door behind them closing.

"What's a rim queen?" Mathews asked as they walked.

"Can't be explained in words," Jackie answered with no expression on his face. "I'd have to demonstrate it for you."

Mathews remained curious, but discretion got the best of him. "Maybe some other time," he answered.

The door at the other end of the hall opened for them immediately, admitting them into a spacious and luxurious waiting room of sorts. "Where are we?" Craig asked, amazed to find himself in a room that would have served any penthouse well.

"Specifically, just about the center of the park," Jackie explained. "Or, if you didn't mean geographically, we're now at the local office of C.A.M.P."

"Isn't this rather a dangerous place for it," Craig asked. "Looks to me like it would be touchy to get in and out of."

"Not at all," Jackie assured him. "In the first place, that park is the sort of place where no one would question seeing a homosexual, or even question it if he seems to have disappeared. As you saw, the opening would be impossible to find accidentally, and if it were found, no one would get beyond the first entrance. In any case, there is even another entrance. It opens from one of the sewers under Pennsylvania Avenue, and that can be reached from a nearby building. So you see, everything is taken care of."

Mathews had to admit it was certainly a more complex organization than he had originally imagined. "Now what?" he asked, glancing around. They were alone in the office, and so far no one had approached them.

"Oh, you'll have to have a seat. You'll find a bar behind that folding screen over there, and there should be hot coffee also. I'll take this note in and let them get started on it."

While Craig poured himself a cup of coffee, Jackie disappeared through another door. He returned a few minutes later and poured brandy for himself, taking a seat facing Craig.

"This must be quite an outfit," Craig said after a moment of silence. "I didn't realize it was so big an operation."

"Few people do," Jackie said quietly. "In fact, few know of its existence—but that makes our work easier, so we don't mind."

"But you're sort of a policeman for fag...for homosexuals, aren't you? How can you do any good for them if they don't know you exist? They can't very well report things to you."

"Oh, they do, in various ways. There are people who know of us, in the first place. The leaders in the homophile movement, agents who work undercover in strategic jobs—some of them with police departments. And there are the regular news media, that give us information on things happening around the world, particularly anything that appears to be organized and large scale."

"So when any homosexual runs into a problem, you're there, is what you're saying?"

"Well, we can't of course be on hand for every crime involving a homosexual, nor would I want to be. Let's face it, many homosexuals go around constantly asking for trouble. If it were only their own lives involved, then it would be only their own personal business, but they make things worse for all of us. On the other hand, homosexuals are too often the innocent victims of unscrupulous people. That's were our interests lie. And I doubt that much goes on in the world of the homosexual that is not known to High Camp. Without trying to detail the sort of information kept on file, High Camp's records include full histories of some five million homosexuals throughout the world."

Craig was impressed. "I would never have guessed there were that many."

Jackie grinned and shrugged. "Those are only the known ones, although the fact that they're known to us doesn't mean they're notorious. Some of them are at the absolute top of the governmental levels."

"Well, I must say your outfit is impressive. But tell me, where did it come from? How did it get started?"

"No one really knows for sure. Legend has it that the original founder of the organization was a man who was enormously wealthy and powerful in one of the Midwestern states. Among other things, he had managed to have a friend of his put in charge of the local state police. Both of them had lovers, the sweet young thing type."

"One night the two younger ones, who both went to evening classes, were leaving the library after doing some studying together. The park surrounding the library was quite a hangout for rough trade, and the two were accosted by a gang of young punks—dirt, we call them. They got badly beaten, and robbed. As the story goes, their two older lovers were angry, and decided together to set up a vigilante team, to watch over that park. They kept a constant string of husky young homosexuals there, to clean it up."

"I'd never thought of young homosexuals as being husky—or guard material, for that matter."

"They can be. These were," Jackie said.

"But that still doesn't explain the name of your organization."

"Ah, yes. Well, the ones who guarded that original park were said to be camping, because they all but lived there. Anyway, it worked well, and in short order the park was cleaned up.

"Meaning, it was made safe for fairies to cruise in," Mathews said.

"It was made safe for anyone, gay or straight, who wanted to walk there. The entire city benefited from what these two men had done. Anyway, they decided they might be happier if they devoted themselves to that sort of thing in the future. The one had the money, the other was highly trained in police work. They approached a few more friends, experts in various fields—the idea caught on like wildfire—and here we are now."

Craig shook his head. It was an incredible story and yet, sitting here in this underground hideout, only yards away from the White House itself and yet undetected by the sharpest agents who watched the area, to say nothing of the local police, he couldn't help being impressed.

"And you?" Craig asked finally. "How did you get into this?"

"Oh, that's easy," Jackie said with a reminiscent smile. "I had a crush on someone, my idol. He became the victim of a blackmailer, and finally took his life, after losing everything. When I was approached by C.A.M.P., I wasn't much more than a child, but I jumped at the chance to become an agent."

A red light began blinking on and off over the door to the inner offices, cutting short Jackie's dissertation. "They've got something for me," Jackie said, standing and heading for the door. "Be back in a minute."

He was smiling triumphantly when he returned a minute later.

"How are they doing with it?" Craig asked, without

much hope.

"Oh, great," Jackie said. "They've got it all translated for us."

Craig was unable to believe what he had heard. "You mean they decoded that damned thing already? My boys worked on it for hours, without any luck at all."

Jackie handed him a typed sheet, with the translated message.

"The assassination will take place as scheduled, on Friday," Craig read aloud. He glanced up, his eyes worried. "This is big," he said. "That much is obvious. But whose assassination?"

Jackie shrugged. "That's all there was to the note. But this is Monday already—check that, Tuesday morning, and we're going to have to get busy if we're going to do anything to prevent it."

"There's one place we can safely start," Craig said, standing grimly. "That poodle parlor that the note came from. I think it's safe to say that's a front for the Butterfly operation."

"What about all those warrants and things we'll need," Jackie asked. "Of course, if I were working on my own, I wouldn't bother with them."

"Neither will I," Craig said. "I'll worry about protocol later, but for now I don't want those snakes to get away from us while we're being polite."

Jackie led the way out of the underground hideout. In

the first chamber inside, he used a periscope to assure that the coast was clear above before letting them out.

Minutes later, they were once again strolling through Lafayette Park.

* * * * * * *

The poodle parlor was not far from Aunt Lily's home. It was dark, which was to be expected at this hour of night. Jackie and Craig looked over the front, and then circled around to the back that opened into an alley. This was darker and a less conspicuous place to enter than the street.

"We'll have to force the lock," Mathews said as he tried the door stealthily.

"That might give anyone inside a warning of our approach, if there is anyone inside." Jackie stooped down and examined the lock. It was not a particularly difficult one, quite simple in fact in design.

He removed a small mechanism from his pocket, a collection of wires of varied sizes, twisted in various shapes. He tried first one, and then another of the "picks". There was a telltale click, and the door opened for him.

Mathews said nothing, but as he led the way into the dark interior, he was making some revision to his opinion regarding the small, blond agent with him. Queer or not, Jackie was one hell of a sharp operator.

Craig was beginning to feel that Jackie was the one person he would most like to have about in a pinch.

Mathews drew a gun from his shoulder holster. Jackie, he noticed, was not armed, and Craig discreetly led the way down a short, dark hallway. They paused when they reached the door at the end. The room beyond could be empty and harmless—or they could be walking into a hornet's nest.

Jackie tapped Craig's shoulder and gave him a "let me" gesture. Craig was dubious, but at Jackie's insistent nod, he stepped aside. With one hand, Jackie quietly but quickly twisted the knob and shoved the door open a few inches. With the other, he tossed something inside. A second later there was a quick puff of smoke and a flash of light. Jackie closed the door quickly and grinned at Craig's puzzled face.

"Harmless, but effective in putting anyone to sleep," he explained. "If there was anyone inside, they won't give us any trouble now."

They waited a moment longer before Jackie nodded that it was safe now for them to go inside. "The gas dissipates rapidly," he said, opening the door.

Their caution, however, had not been necessary. There was no one inside the room, nor in the main shop beyond it. What's more, it was evident that whoever might have been here earlier in the day was gone and would not be coming back. The place had been stripped bare.

"They must have realized that they mixed up the dogs," Craig said, looking around in disappointment. "They bolted."

Jackie said nothing, although he too was disappointed. He had hoped to be in on a rare arrest of Butterfly personnel. There was still another problem to be considered, however, beyond their individual chagrin.

Someone was going to be assassinated. They didn't know who, or when, or how, only that it was going to happen. And without a lead to go on, it was unlikely they could do anything to prevent it.

* * * * * * *

It was not much before dawn by the time Craig dropped Jackie off at Aunt Lily's home in one of the older sections of the city. Mathews was obviously tired and disappointed by the evening's outcome. Jackie too was sorry that their efforts had not been more successful. Unlike Mathews, however, he was not yet showing any signs of weariness. As an agent for C.A.M.P., he was accustomed to keeping long and irregular hours. If need be, he could easily continue on at full steam for another day, or longer.

The house was dark except for a light at the front door, and another one shining dimly in the front hall.

Jackie removed his shoes and carried them as he went up the gracefully curved stairway, searching his memory for the location of Honey's room. He remembered, and found it without any difficulty.

Honey was sleeping soundly, as he had expected. His bed was an elaborate, canopied affair, feminine and luxurious. In the midst of the silk sheets and brocaded coverlets, Honey had kicked the coverings from his body and was curled up invitingly. In the moonlight that filtered through the window, his gamin-like body gleamed with alabaster whiteness. He wore a pair of very scant briefs that appeared to be silk also, and, so far as Jackie could tell in the light, were pink, or maybe pale lavender.

There was nothing feminine, however, about the enormous bulge that lifted the front of the briefs ceilingward, even in its relaxed stage. Jackie eyed the tempting outline hungrily, but courtesy held him in check. It would be thoughtless to awaken Honey at this hour, when such matters could wait until morning.

Suppressing his disappointment, Jackie pulled his eyes away from the enchanting vista, and began to undress. The body that was gradually exposed to the moonlight was a paradox, as Jackie himself was in many ways. Like Honey, Jackie was sometimes effeminate to the extreme. In Jackie's case, however, this was only another of the roles that he assumed when it was convenient for his work—an effeminate homosexual was less likely to be suspected of being an agent, and was not so feared. When it was necessary, however, Jackie could quickly discard all such mannerisms, and could appear as masculine as anyone. With him, it was a matter of conscious choice.

His appearance was equally deceptive. He was small and slender, and the casual observer would no doubt regard him as weak and helpless. In fact, Jackie was far from either condition. His limbs, although small, were molded of sheer, rocklike muscle. Combined with a strength that could almost be described as super-human, was a speed and agility that never failed to confound his enemies. He could move like greased lightening—he had run the mile in just about half of the world's record, and that with no effort. There were few if any sports in which he did not excel. Superfag, he had once been described by one of his associates, and indeed the name was not far from the truth.

Naked, he stretched lazily before dropping to the floor and rapidly executing a few hundred pushups, alternating from one hand to the other. It was a policy that he never failed to exercise at least slightly each day, to insure that he would stay in top-notch condition. In his business, being out of condition could mean going out of business, the hard way.

Finally, with a last wistful glance at Honey's

briefs, he crawled into bed and stretched out on his back, staring up at the flower-print canopy above as he thought over the day's events, and considered the question of his return to Los Angeles. There was not much he could accomplish here, and by all rights he should be on his way back. On the other hand, it had been a while since he allowed himself a day off. He had checked for messages while at the C.A.M.P. office earlier, and learned from Rich that things were quiet on the West Coast. And Rich knew where to get in touch with him if anything came up.

His thoughts changed directions quite suddenly. A second later, all thought of Rich, the West Coast, or C.A.M.P., were completely gone from his mind, and he was aware of only one thing...the warm, strong, very-much-awake hand that had slid across his stomach and taken firm hold of him.

Never unprepared, his flesh responded instantly and totally, rising to the occasion admirably. Beside him on the bed, Jackie heard Honey giggle delightedly at the instant results.

"I thought you were asleep," Jackie whispered, rolling over on his side and reaching for his companion.

"I was," Honey said, coming into Jackie's arms without hesitation. "But a man's body will wake me up every time. My one nostril twitches whenever one gets within two feet of me."

"What a crazy burglar alarm," Jackie decided. He was prevented from making further comment by the ripe fullness of Honey's mouth glued hotly to his. Honey, he decided at once, was a honey—sweet and smooth, brewed from the loveliest and most fragrant of blossoms. He kicked himself mentally as he thought how available Honey had been to him all along, and he had never done anything about it before.

"You know," he whispered, nibbling Honey's ear. "When I saw you five years ago, you were only fifteen, and a gangly, bad-complexioned brat."

"You should know better than to judge a fruit before it's ripe," Honey told him.

Jackie's hand had invaded the rear area of those briefs. They were silk, all right, and they very quickly allowed him access to the warm, sweet flesh beneath. This was one fruit, Jackie told himself happily, that was now plenty ripe.

"If you don't take those damned things off me," Honey said. "They're going to be ripped in two soon."

Jackie allowed himself to feel in front. It was true, the briefs were certainly being stretched beyond their reasonable capacity. Always sympathetic, Jackie chose to alleviate the sufferings of the fabric. He clasped the elastic in his fingers and slid it downward, over the hips that Honey lifted to make the task easier. Jackie's mouth was following the fabric, although when he reached the open plains of Honey's flat abdomen, his mouth fell behind.

He inched his way slowly downward, an ocean of soft, curly hair tickling his nose, and finally he collided with Honey's answer to the Washington Monument. In the dark, it didn't seem much different from the original, and skilled though he was in such matters, Jackie doubted he would be able to manage it all. Still, he could think of nothing more delightful than making the attempt.

Stiff problem that it was, Jackie made a determined effort to absorb it deeply, with a degree of success that promised him real fulfillment in the not too distant future. For the moment, however, he wanted to taste all of the rich harvest before him. He explored to the very root of the subject and then beyond, the path lying open to him. He reached his goal, and lingered there to make a penetrating analysis before Honey's squirming and moaning warned him that he best not delay.

In a twinkling, Jackie was back to his original location, and with no regrets at having been summoned there. He had always disliked catching cold, but he never complained about having something in his throat. Nor did he mind in the least when Honey decided to occupy himself. They held tightly to one another, their bodies moving in see-saw fashion, and Jackie could only be grateful that he did not have to dine alone.

It was short and frantic. Honey's mouth and tongue were as skilled as his anatomy was satisfying. Jackie soared upward into the heavens and, as he exploded in his delight, it felt as though the top were being blown off his head.

He was aware of the fact that Honey was right there with him, joining him flood for flood—but most important, or at least most prominent in Jackie's consciousness, was the realization that he had, at the very last, surmounted Everest, so to speak. Except that, where mountain climbers crowed about reaching the top, Jackie was as proud as any of them to have reached the bottom. In the morning, he would probably be sore, but for the moment he felt mighty like the canary that had claimed the cat. Furthermore, he had answered his own questions about returning to Los Angeles, or remaining here for a few days. He planned on a great deal of visiting before going.

CHAPTER SIX

IT WAS LATE MORNING BY the time Jackie awoke. He opened his eyes to see that he had not been dreaming the night before after all, as he had momentarily supposed. There, only inches from his face, was the same pulsing source of delight that had provided him such pleasure. Jackie stared at it briefly, managing to raise his eyes only with some effort. Honey was awake, and grinning down at him.

"Just saving breakfast for you," Honey announced, edging closer.

There was nothing Jackie liked better than breakfast in bed. As a result, it was nearly noon by the time he and Honey ventured downstairs. Aunt Lily greeted them pleasantly, and insisted on bringing fresh coffee into the breakfast room for them, and even joining them.

"I've been doing a lot of thinking," she said as she seated herself between the two young men. "I mean, it's been so exciting being involved in international espionage—just like in a James Bond thriller, don't you see."

"Well, Aunt Lily," Jackie said, smiling tolerantly at her over his coffee cup. "I'm afraid it never comes out quite as simple as in those books. It's actually a very difficult and dangerous business."

"I know, but it's exciting. Anyway, I've been wondering why we couldn't do more of the same. Not you, of course, I know you're already involved in the field, and I wouldn't dream of crowding in your territory. But it looks to me like there's spying enough to go around. And I think this household needs some activity, something to spice up our lives a little."

"I think you're right," Honey agreed, to Jackie's further concern. "Things do get awfully dull around here. But let us get one coded message, and already we've had two gorgeous agents hanging around the place."

"Thanks for the two compliments," Jackie said with a grin.

"Two?"

"That I'm gorgeous, and that I'm here."

"Now, boys," Aunt Lily interrupted. "Don't try to get me off the subject. I've already spoken to Nasturtia, and Mari, and even Gladiola, and they all think it's a nice idea. So we've decided to have a secret meeting, tonight at midnight."

"A secret meeting? And at midnight?" Jackie was

scarcely able to conceal his amusement. "Why all the mystery?"

"Because I've read all those books, and I know that's the way things are done. Now don't you worry, I'll take care of all the details. Of course, you wouldn't really have to come, Jackie, but we'd like you there anyway, just to see for yourself how us amateurs can do."

"I'd be delighted," Jackie assured her. "Where do I go?"

"The basement, in the furnace room," Aunt Lily told him. "At the stroke of twelve. And be careful you're not being followed."

* * * * * * *

It was shortly before the stroke of twelve that Honey woke Jackie from his sleep. Jackie had, in fact, been asleep only a short while, although he and Honey had come to bed about nine in the evening. There had been more interesting things to attend to, however, than sleep.

"You mean the meeting is still on," Jackie asked drowsily, reaching for a pair of trousers. "I thought everyone would have forgotten about it by now."

"I think it's very exciting," Honey informed him. "Just think, we may be a big thing internationally."

"I don't think the world is ready for you," Jackie said frankly, but he softened the remark with a grin and a playful grab at Honey's legs.

* * * * * * *

Surprisingly enough, the others were there—all except Nasturtia. Mari was sent for her, and returned in a few minutes to announce that Aunt Nasturtia was on her way.

"She'd forgotten about it," Mari explained, "Thought it was tomorrow night anyway."

While they waited, Jackie glanced about the dimly-lighted room. The windows high up on the walls had been covered with burlap, and Aunt Lily had placed candles about with eerie results.

"What is that?" Jackie asked, pointed to the one wall. The faded portrait could not have looked more out of place, but even more preposterous was the fact that a hole had been cut in the old gentleman's chest, and through it protruded the lens of an antiquated camera.

"A hidden camera," Aunt Lily explained in a very matter-of-fact tone. Jackie did not pursue the subject further.

Aunt Nasturtia arrived soon, and the meeting was ready to begin. Jackie toyed with Honey's sizable charms as he listened to Aunt Lily's opening remarks. The excitement of spying was discussed, and it was agreed that all had enjoyed their brief episode, and would enjoy more such sport. Jackie did not have the heart to tell them that it wasn't all such fun. In any event, he was convinced that merely contemplating spying would keep them happily occupied for a few days.

"Now," Aunt Lily was saying, obviously enjoying her role as ringleader. "I've chosen a name for our organization. We're going to call ourselves WATERCRESS."

"WATERCRESS?" Honey repeated.

"I think it's charming," Nasturtia offered.

"What does it mean?" Mari wanted to know.

"Women Acting Together, Enlightened, Righteous, Courageous, Responsible, Enterprising, Strong, and Sensible."

"But that's silly," Honey protested with a pout. "You didn't say anything about me. I'm not a woman."

Mari giggled, but Aunt Lily silenced her with a frown. "Well, darling, can't you see, we can't very well spell WATERCRESS with an M-it wouldn't come out right. You'll just have to be sort of a silent partner."

"I still don't like it," Honey grumbled.

"I think it's cute," Mari decided. Jackie avoided making any comment. After all, it wasn't his party.

"Besides," Aunt Lily went on. "We'll make it up to you by giving you one of the more important roles in the organization. We're going to make you our signal man."

"What's that?"

"The man who gives signals, of course. Every secret organization has to have a communication system of some kind, and a code, just like Butterfly. Well, ours is going to be music."

"Music?" Honey sounded dubious, but somewhat more interested.

"Of course. We'll have various pieces of music which each have a specific meaning. When you want to give us a message, you just play the 'Moonlight Sonata' to tell us of danger."

"I only know the first movement," Honey reminded her.

"I'm sure that's all we'd need," Aunt Lily insisted. "By the time you get that played, we should have gotten the message."

"But that's the only piece I know."

"Well, then, you'll just have to learn some new ones, and inform us of what each one means."

Honey seemed pacified by that explanation, and lapsed into thoughtful silence, not even noticing Jackie's hand which was still busy on Honey's lap.

The rest of the meeting was free of much argument, although this may have been accounted for in part by the fact that Nasturtia and Gladiola were both asleep by now. Aunt Lily herself would assume the responsibility of finding an outlet for their services.

She shot Jackie a hopeful glance, but he shook his

head. He did not think C.A.M.P. would particularly welcome the efforts of WATERCRESS as a partner. He could hardly wait, however, to see Craig Mathews' reaction to the news. And at the thought of the handsome Irishman, Jackie felt a quickening of his pulse. He began to wish for Aunt Lily to cut her explanation short. Of a sudden, he was in a hurry to get back to bed, although he was not in the least sleepy.

* * * * * * *

Late in the morning, Jackie paid a visit to the C.I.A. His excuse was a curiosity regarding any subsequent developments, although his real purpose was merely to see Craig again. Regrettably, Craig was out. Eventually he was greeted by a rather flirtatious Miss Temple, who proved to be the secretary of the C.I.A. chief himself.

Miss Temple, one of the antiseptically pretty breed of women who somehow manage to find themselves in the government service, was more than a little interested in Jackie, which he found peculiar. She certainly would know who he was, that he worked for a homosexual organization and was presumably himself homosexual.

But then, he reminded himself wearily, many women liked that—they seemed to regard it as a challenge, and fed their egos with the satisfaction of diverting a boy's interest from males to themselves. In this case, however, she was wasting her time. Jackie had been normal far too long to become interested in the opposite sex now. He left a message for Craig, which he doubted would be delivered, and prepared to leave.

"If you happen to be watching television this afternoon, you'll see Craig, and me also," Miss Temple offered as Jackie reached the door.

He paused briefly. "Not a quiz show, I hope."

Miss Temple laughed, a terribly phony sound. "Oh no, just an appearance by our boss. I'll be with him at the luncheon. I'm afraid Craig will be harder to spot, since he'll be mingling unostentatiously in the crowd, but if you look you should be able to spot him."

Jackie thanked her and left.

* * * * * * *

He arrived back at Aunt Lily's house to find that her day had been no more productive than his. She had attempted to call both the U.S. State Department, and the Russian Embassy, with absolutely no success at either address.

"They wouldn't even talk to me," Aunt Lily snorted angrily. "Not even when I explained that we were spies, and looking for work. I even asked at the Russian Embassy if we couldn't buy some little piece of information, just to get ourselves started."

Jackie smiled and offered her consolation. Finally

he made his way upstairs to Honey's room. Enjoyable though his visit was, he knew that he would soon have to be returning to Los Angeles. Rich had kindly not contacted him with any assignments, but he knew that merely meant his partner was burdening himself with extra work. He would have liked to become better acquainted with Craig, of course, but that seemed an unlikely possibility. In the long run, it would probably be wiser if he began his packing and made ready to depart.

His efforts were interrupted, however, by Aunt Nasturtia's appearance in the room. She burst in without knocking, a fact in itself unusual.

"You've got to come down and look at the television," she sputtered, tugging at his arm wildly. "Come quickly, oh, please."

"The television?" Jackie was bewildered by her actions, but he allowed himself to be piloted down the stairs toward the den, where the older model television set was kept, hidden from the sight of guests.

As he entered the room and saw the luncheon scene on view, he remembered Miss Temple's remarks at the C.I.A. offices earlier.

"Oh, yes," he said aloud, a little annoyed that Aunt Nasturtia should have made such a big thing out of Craig's appearance on television. "Craig is on this afternoon."

"No, not him," Aunt Nasturtia was saying, pointing hysterically at the screen. Aunt Lily was there too, and she seemed every bit as excited. "The woman!"

"The woman?" The only woman on the screen at the moment was Miss Temple herself, seated dutifully at the side of her boss.

"That's her," Aunt Nasturtia explained in an excited voice. "That's the woman with the other white poodle!"

Jackie suddenly understood the reason for all the excitement. "You mean the one at the poodle parlor, the one whose dog they got mixed up with Fritz?"

"That's her, I'm positive."

Jackie stared dumfounded at Miss Temple's bland face on the screen. If Aunt Nasturtia was correct in her identification...and if the note they had intercepted had really been intended for the other white poodle...then Miss Temple was an agent for Butterfly! It was incredible, the secretary to the chief of the C.I.A.—and yet, it was possible.

"Whew," he gasped, seating himself. "This could be something really big. I have a feeling I'd better get in touch with Craig, and right away."

"Jackie, dear." It was Aunt Lily who delayed him, tugging at his sleeve gently but firmly. "There's just one thing. It is our discovery, you remember."

Jackie nodded reluctantly, already suspecting what was coming next, and not knowing how to prevent it.

"Well then, I want you to promise us that WATERCRESS will be in on the case."

"Aunt Lily, I can't promise anything like that. For one thing, it isn't even my case. It's a C.I.A. matter, and they might not even want me butting in."

"Well then, promise me you'll at least ask that nice young man, Mr. Mathews. If you ask him, I'm sure he'll let us help. That's all we want to do, really. We have no intention of taking his job away from him."

Jackie sighed. "I'll try, Aunt Lily. But be prepared, if you do get to help, to find that it may be very dull and very routine work. You'll be acting as flunkies, if anything."

"Oh, we'll be thrilled to do anything at all," Aunt Lily promised him, all smiles and happiness again.

Just how he should go about turning this case over to the C.I.A. remained something of a puzzle to Jackie. He could hardly go to the chief, since that would mean going through Miss Temple, and perhaps tipping her off to the details. Craig was decidedly the best bet, but he would have to see Craig privately. With that in mind, he telephoned and left a message for Craig to contact him, adding that it was urgent.

That brought a suggestion that someone else handle the matter, which Jackie declined, and a request for information regarding the problem, which Jackie again declined. The young man on the other end of the line sounded both disappointed and annoyed by the time the conversation was ended.

Nevertheless, Craig did call, in the middle of the afternoon. Jackie explained that he could not go into details over the phone and, although Craig sounded dubious, he finally agreed to meet Jackie for a drink later in the afternoon.

* * * * * * *

At first, Craig was cold and distant, as he had been at their first meeting. As Jackie explained, quickly and efficiently, the situation that had developed, Craig lost his aloofness and became all attention.

"Miss Temple?" he said finally, aghast. "But that's not possible...or is it...?"

Jackie allowed him to contemplate the matter for a moment or two before going on. "As you can see for yourself, it's a touchy situation. One could hardly make a charge without being absolutely certain of being able to prove it. Personally, I think it would be well worth your while to investigate it, strictly on the Q.T. That way, if nothing comes of it, you haven't caused any embarrassment for yourself, or for anybody else. And if it all checks out, then it will be a fine feather in your cap."

"You're right, of course." Craig was frowning thoughtfully as he swirled his drink about in his glass.

"But I'll need some help."

Jackie said nothing, waiting for the handsome agent to continue.

"I'm not too keen on your outfit, or on your kind. I guess you know that." Craig softened the remark with an apologetic, heart-melting grin. His Irish eyes were smiling, and just like the song they were stealing Jackie's heart away.

"Still, I have to admit you're a sharp operator," Craig continued. "What do you say, how about giving me a hand with this one, at least until I've something definite to go on?"

Jackie remembered his promise to Aunt Lily. He hated to involve his zany relatives in the case at all, but he couldn't go back on his word—and anyway, it was entirely possible they might be useful. After all, until they had a definite case, he and Craig would be working on their own.

"It's a deal," he said finally. "But on one condition."

"What's that?"

"You have to let my aunts and cousins help too." Ignoring Craig's dismayed expression, Jackie explained quickly about WATERCRESS and its intended functions, and about his promise to Aunt Lily.

"They can't hurt anything," he finished. "And I've a feeling we might need their help."

"All right," Craig gave in finally. "But I have a

feeling myself. I have a feeling we'll both regret this before it's all over."

CHAPTER SEVEN

AS IT DEVELOPED, THE two agents were to need the help of WATERCRESS sooner than expected. In discussing their plans, it soon became evident to Jackie and Craig that the first step would be to check out Miss Temple. If there was an assassination plot underway, and the message had been intended for her, then that was the logical way to begin foiling the plot.

It was obvious, however, that neither Jackie nor Craig, both of whom were known to her, could attempt to do any snooping. That meant calling in someone else to help.

"I still don't like it," Craig objected as they discussed the plan that Jackie had come up with. "Your aunts are both charming ladies, I'm sure, but I don't think either one of them has the brains to accomplish anything for us. Even if they did, it's just too dangerous a job to send them out on."

"We don't have much choice," Jackie pointed out to him. "Someone has got to get inside Miss Temple's apartment and see what can be found there. Neither one of us could get away with it; and besides, as long as Aunt Lily and Aunt Nasturtia are posing as cosmetic salesladies, I don't see that there'll be too much danger for them. Just to be on the safe side, I'll equip them with warning signals, and hang around outside. If anything goes wrong, they can always let me know and I can be there in time to prevent anything from happening."

"I guess you're right," Craig admitted begrudgingly. "But I still don't have much faith in them."

Although he would not admit to them before Craig, Jackie too had his doubts. Fond as he was of his aunts, he knew them to be scatterbrained and silly, dangerous traits in the spying profession. Still, as he had argued, they were the most likely prospects for getting inside Miss Temple's apartment and "casing" the place.

Aunt Lily and Aunt Nasturtia, however, were quite confident, and excited beyond compare. The plan was a simple one. They were to appear at Miss Temple's door as saleswomen, and talk their way inside. Once there, Aunt Nasturtia would create a diversion by fainting. While Miss Temple was helping with Nasturtia, Lily would have her opportunity to look around for anything of particular interest.

"But what exactly will I be looking for?" Aunt Lily asked when the plan had been discussed.

"That's the difficult part," Jackie answered. "I don't know myself. You'll have to use your own judgment, and just look for anything that looks really out of the ordinary."

He gave her a large corsage to be pinned to the bodice of her dress. "It's a camera," he explained, showing her the mechanism concealed in the artificial blossoms. "When you get inside the door, just touch this switch, and it will start filming. It will continue automatically for an hour."

"Oh, how exciting."

"Just remember to start it when you get inside," he reminded her. He also gave each of them small, trivial-looking lockets to be worn about their necks on small gold chains. "These are alarms. If anything goes wrong, break the chain with a quick yank. That'll bring me running from outside."

* * * * * * *

A short time later, Jackie was seated in a car outside the apartment building in which Miss Temple lived. He had dropped Aunt Lily and Aunt Nasturtia two blocks away, so that they would not be seen with him. That effort was wasted, however, for as they approached on the sidewalk, Aunt Nasturtia saw him and waved cheerfully. Jackie groaned inwardly and looked away, hoping Miss Temple had not been at her window to see the action.

Nasturtia was fairly bubbling over with excitement

as they went up in the elevator. Aunt Lily, however, had grown nervous now that the moment was at hand. She actually jumped when the door opened in response to her knock, and Miss Temple herself stood before them.

"Savon calling," Lily managed to chirp, swallowing weakly.

"We've come to show you how you too can be beautiful," Nasturtia added with a toothy smile.

Miss Temple surveyed the two of them. "You should practice what you preach," she said coldly, starting to close the door.

Aunt Lily recovered her senses in time to block the closing of the door with one foot. "Oh, we won't take but a minute of your time, and we do have some wonderful things to show you."

"Would it matter in the least if I promised to believe it?" Miss Temple asked sarcastically. She was trying to force the door closed, but Aunt Lily had taken advantage of an opportunity to squeeze halfway inside. Now she was stubbornly holding her ground.

"Oh, all right," Miss Temple surrendered finally, opening the door so quickly that Aunt Lily all but fell into the room. "But make it quick, will you?"

The two swept triumphantly into the room. Aunt Lily's eyes were everywhere, darting about in search of any clue she might find. Miss Temple had crossed the room to pour herself a drink from a crystal decanter.

"Psst," Aunt Nasturtia asked in a loud stage whisper that would easily have carried for blocks, "did you remember the camera?"

Miss Temple looked up with her eyes wide. "What was that?" she demanded sharply.

Aunt Lily shot a ferocious glance at Nasturtia, and sought desperately for an explanation. "Oh, I'm afraid my *assistant* is a bit presumptuous. You see, we sometimes carry a camera with us when we're demonstrating Savon cosmetics, so that we can take before-and-after pictures. But I'm sure that's hardly the sort of thing you'd want to participate in."

"Hardly," Miss Temple agreed. Although her tone was dry, she at least seemed to accept the explanation, to Aunt Lily's relief. With Miss Temple watching her so closely, however, Aunt Lily had not yet had an opportunity to start the camera. Heaven only knew what important clues she was passing by.

According to the plan, it should have been time for Nasturtia to faint. There was scarcely time for this to be attempted, however, before the doorbell rang again. Miss Temple glowered at it and at her two unwelcome guests before she went to answer it.

Aunt Lily could not see who was at the door, but the voices carried clearly.

"Important message," a male voice explained. "It's from Bigelow himself."

Aunt Lily's pulse quickened as she realized they might have arrived at a highly crucial moment. She strained her ears to hear more, but the conversation was rudely interrupted by the fact that Aunt Nasturtia did pick that precise moment, after all, to faint.

"Oh, Nasturtia," Aunt Lily wailed, fighting down an urge to kick her sister bodily. "Get off that floor."

Miss Temple had returned from the door, and the messenger was gone—and as if things weren't bad enough, Lily discovered that Nasturtia was not acting. She had really and truly fainted!

"Oh," she wailed loudly, "she really has fainted"

"Well you surely didn't think she was just taking a nap, did you?" Miss Temple asked with sarcasm. "Maybe I should get her some water."

It would have been an ideal time to look about the room, except that, in her concern for her sister, Aunt Lily tried to loosen Nasturtia's blouse, and managed instead to break the slender chain that held the little locket.

"Oh, dear," she gasped as she realized the alarm would be sounding downstairs, summoning Jackie to the rescue.

Miss Temple had returned with a glass of water. Abandoning decorum, Aunt Lily tossed it into Nasturtia's face. Nasturtia revived quickly, sputtering and gasping like a fish out of water.

"Come on," Lily ordered, virtually dragging the other woman to her feet. "We're finished here."

With Miss Temple staring after them in bewilderment, they fled from the apartment, down the hall and into the arms of Jackie, who was indeed on his way to rescue them.

All in all, Jackie concluded as he heard Aunt Lily's sobbing explanation, it had not been a very successful attempt at espionage.

* * * * * * *

"Well, it wasn't a total loss," Craig sympathized when the group had returned to the house. "We at least learned that someone higher up than Miss Temple is called Bigelow."

"But there must be hundreds of Bigelows in the city," Jackie pointed out. "How do we find out which one it is that we want?"

"There's only eleven," Craig said with a grin. "And we find out the hard way—by checking out each one of them."

"Oh, then we'll still be needed," Lily said with obvious relief.

Jackie frowned in Craig's direction. He was genuinely sorry he had allowed the others to become involved at all; but Aunt Lily was correct—it would save a lot of time if they all checked out the Bigelows in the city.

* * * * * * *

Honey and Gladiola went together. Honey did not feel quite safe by himself, and it was the consensus of opinion that Gladiola was not bright enough to attempt anything by herself.

The rotting old boarding house before which they found themselves certainly lent itself to an undercover operation. Somewhat isolated from the other houses in the none-too-respectable neighborhood, and exuding an aura of disrepute, it looked the sort of place that would spawn evil of any sort.

"How do you suppose we should go about this?" Honey asked as they lingered outside. Their instructions had been merely to meet the Bigelow at this address, if possible, and size him up as a possible agent.

Gladiola screwed up her face thoughtfully; it was evident that mental concentration was no small effort for her. "I don't see why we couldn't just explain to them who we are, and ask them open-like if they are the ones we are looking for."

Honey sighed and rolled his eyes. "Oh, no, that would never do, even I know that. I suppose we'll just have to play it by ear, so to speak."

The house itself offered them one possibility; it bore a sign advertising rooms for rent. If all else failed,

Honey decided they could use that as an excuse to get inside.

The ringing of the antiquated doorbell was answered after a long pause by a rather sleazy and plump blonde in a red kimono that was only slightly more faded than she was. A cigarette dangled from her smeared mouth, and she squinted through the smoke to study them suspiciously.

"Yeah?" she asked finally in a nasal voice.

"Mr. Bigelow?" Honey asked timidly. He had little experience in such matters, but this looked to him like what Aunt Lily described as a "painted woman."

"Whatdoyawant?" the blonde growled in one breath, the cigarette bobbing as her lips moved.

Honey hesitated. Surely this wasn't Mr. Bigelow? But then, no one had really said that it had to be a mister. And if this was Miss Bigelow, then this was the person he wanted to talk to.

"I'm here to talk business," he said in a lower voice that he hoped was appropriately conspiratorial. "I think you know what I mean."

The blonde eyed him slowly, looking him up and down, and then took a minute longer to study Gladiola, who bristled slightly in indignation.

"Yeah, I guess I do," she admitted finally. "But we better not talk out here."

Honey gave Gladiola a triumphant wink. That

remark certainly suggested underground activities, clandestine doings. Happily, he followed the blonde inside, Gladiola tagging along behind.

"Who'd you say sent you?" the blonde asked when they were in the dim, musty hallway.

Honey moved still closer to her and whispered "Butterfly."

"Ah, go on." The blonde did not appear at all certain whether or not she should take him seriously. "Don't kid an old bag."

"I wouldn't kid you—any more than Miss Temple would."

"Shirley Temple?" His hostess was aghast. "Look, we specialize in variety here, but I ain't got nobody of that type. Give me another try, okay? What would you like?"

The conversation seemed, to Honey, to be growing rapidly more confusing. "Butterfly," he repeated in a more emphatic tone.

The blonde shook her head and gave him a disappointed look. "Boy, I've had 'em in here, they wanted a cow, or a sheep—once even a boa constrictor. But you're the first one ever went the butterfly route. Come on now, you're puttin' me on, nobody's that small. You're teasing me."

Honey stubbornly shook his head no. He was convinced he was on the track now, and he would not be dissuaded.

The blonde shrugged. "Okay, Charlie. Male or female butterfly?"

Honey was unprepared for that question. His instinct was to answer the former, but this was not a matter of personal pleasure, this was business. "Whoever knows the most," he answered.

"Hell, how should I know how smart it is. Look, have you ever tried 'around the world?' It's pretty great if you never tried it."

Honey had to admit that he had not, but his instinct told him that this was a clue of some sort, perhaps a password. "I'm game for anything," he said with a wicked leer.

"Well, that's better. Why don't I show your Mammy here into the parlor, and you can go up to see Marie. She's our best girl."

"Where he goes, I go," Gladiola declared emphatically, with a tone and an expression that brooked no argument.

The blonde only shook her head in confusion. "That what you want, sonny?"

When Honey nodded, she shrugged philosophically. "If it's okay with Marie, it's okay with me, but it'll cost more. Five bucks for Junior here, and two dollars each for any extra passengers."

Honey and Gladiola exchanged glances. "Will you

excuse us?" Honey said, and piloted Gladiola just out of hearing range. "I've only got five dollars and fifty cents. Can you come up with another dollar and a half?"

"I still don't see what we're paying good money for," Gladiola protested, but she fished a battered change purse from the bodice of her dress and began to count the change it contained.

"Information," Honey explained, counting with her to correct her inevitable mistakes. "Spies always have to buy information."

"Seven dollars ought to buy us one hell of an almanac," Gladiola declared as she handed over the money.

"Room six," the hostess told them when they had paid their fee. "I'll ring the buzzer to let Marie know you're coming up."

Room six proved to be at the top of the stairs. Honey could not disguise his nervousness as they made their way to the door. With each step, they were traveling deeper into what might be the very nerve center of their enemy's operation.

Marie was no more stunning than the blonde downstairs, and even more scantily dressed. She wore only a dingy half slip and a worn, all-but-useless bra that allowed her heavy breasts to dangle nearly to her waist.

She was seated on the edge of the bed as they entered

the room, obviously waiting. When they came in, she showed some surprise at seeing the two of them.

"You together, or is business just booming?"

"We're together," Honey assured her. For that fact he was grateful. There was no telling what might happen next.

Marie did not seem to mind in the least. "Who's first, or do we make it one big party?"

"We have no secrets from one another," Honey explained, indicating Gladiola.

"If that's how you want it. Better take off your clothes, kid, it'll save wear and tear."

Honey was aghast. "My clothes?"

Gladiola was even more indignant. "He can do what he wants, but I ain't takin' off a stitch."

"Me neither," Honey decided.

"Suit yourself. I'll take mine off, if you don't mind." Marie's clothes were few, but she began without any show of modesty to remove them, starting with the bra.

"No!" Honey's face was beet red. "Leave them on, please."

"All of them? Are you sure you don't want me to wrap up in a blanket?"

"I just want to talk to you." Honey's voice was virtually a wail.

"Talk?"

"Yes. We're not the first ones who have come to see

you, are we?"

"Not by a long shot, but you're the first ones who ever wanted to talk."

Despite the fact that she was not too bright, it was Gladiola who began to understand the situation first. A look of comprehension slowly formed on her face as she looked at the puzzled girl, then at Honey.

"Honey," she began finally, grinning. "I think I'm beginning to understand. I think this here is a house of pleasure."

"Well, I don't know if I'd call it that," Marie said drily. "But it's a cat house, if that's what you mean."

"Oh, no." Honey was at a complete loss.

"Oh, yes."

His eyes wide with horror at the thought of what might have happened to him, Honey backed toward the door, ready to bolt when he reached the hall.

"I think you better give her that money," Gladiola said as she followed him more calmly. "After all, we've used a lot of her time, and she is a working woman."

CHAPTER EIGHT

THE LIST OF BIGELOWS was being rapidly shortened, without any appreciable success. Craig felt a bit of hope when he learned that one of them was a butterfly collector, but that proved to be only coincidence.

He returned to the house as agreed, to wait for the others to report. Jackie was checking out the last of the Bigelows, so there was nothing to do now but wait and see.

Mari was there when he arrived. "Any luck?" he asked, without much hope. She shook her head glumly.

"That man I went to see wouldn't have enough sense to come in out of the rain," she told him. "Let alone assassinate anybody."

Craig lit a cigarette and seated himself on the couch. Mari went into the kitchen and returned a moment later with a cup of coffee. She had changed clothes on her return home, donning a filmy negligee that did little to conceal any of her ample charms. She walked with a natural suggestiveness that, despite the fact that she was not Craig's type, he was hard pressed to ignore.

This had been a peculiar case for him anyway, working with not one but two fairies. Not that he found them as repulsive as he had originally expected; the initial shock had worn off quickly. In fact, it was the opposite that was true, and a puzzling new experience. As he was around Jackie and Honey, he was not only becoming accustomed to their mannerisms, but even found that he liked them. In the past he had always thought of such fellows as freaks, and although he read enough to know that they were all around, he had never knowingly associated with any, so that his prejudice had remained intact.

He was beginning to understand that men in prison, or the military service, who were around such men all the time, might weaken and try things that would otherwise be unthinkable for them. Even after such a short time, he was beginning to suspect that his own resistance had weakened somewhat.

It occured to him now, as he watched the indolent swing of Mari's hips crossing the room in front of him, that here was the perfect opportunity to restore his masculine self-image. The bosomy blonde was hardly first class stuff, but unless his judgment was failing, she would probably be a wild romp in the hay. Anyway, he was in a horny mood, and he believed in taking advantage of an opportunity when it presented itself.

"Cigarette?" he asked, giving her the benefit of his nicest little-boy-lost smile.

Mari was appropriately surprised. As a rule, this cute little Irishman was always very cool and aloof toward her. "Sure," she answered, returning the smile with one of her own intended to rapidly melt any ice.

Craig walked over to where she was sitting and handed her a cigarette, lighting it for her. Then, boldly he bent down, tilting her chin up with his hand, and kissed her warmly on the mouth.

She was not the coy type, that much was readily apparent. Mari responded to the kiss by scorching his mouth with her flicking tongue. He shivered as one of her fingers ran lightly up the inside of his leg and brazenly tickled his bashful flesh.

"Looks like we're both in the same mood," he said when the kiss was ended. "Do we have time to go upstairs?"

Mari put out the recently lit cigarette in an ash tray. With one hand, she pulled the negligee open. There was nothing under it but her, naked and luscious. "Why go upstairs?" she asked, leaning back on the love seat. "We can hear them coming in plenty of time."

Any tendency he might have had to argue was quickly overpowered by the view. Unlike some, Mari looked better in the raw than she did clothed.

Her breasts were as huge as they had seemed,

large melon-shaped beauties, but they were firm and youthful, in need of no support or embellishment. The bright cherry-red tips were surrounded by wide, burnt umber circles in sharp contrast to the stark whiteness of her flesh. Her stomach was a gently rounded mound that led the eye downward. It was all climaxed with silken gold, that caught and held Craig's eyes. And, she was a natural blonde

She wasn't waiting for him to agree with her suggestion. He was still staring down at her, licking his lips at the sight, but Mari was already at work. He jumped as he felt her seeking fingers inside his trousers, making their way to him and caressing him hungrily.

He came to her in a hurry. Even the risk of being interrupted only added to his ardor. Mari's velvet thighs opened to him, welcoming his already ardent manhood to her. She moaned with pleasure as he worked avidly, crushing her back against the needlepoint.

There was no romance, no affection, no beauty. It was like two wild animals in desperation, trading flesh for flesh. Mari's hands slid beneath the seat of his trousers, raking the naked skin of his moving buttocks, urging him to greater excess.

It was fast and furious. Craig let go with a white-hot torrent, unable to hold back the finish that rushed from him. He was afraid he had been too quick, but she was ready. The frenzy of his release was all that she needed to reach her own peak, a groaning, shuddering experience that left them both exhausted and drained.

There was the sound of voices from outside, and the rasp of a key in the front door. Craig barely had time to dive for his seat across the room, putting his trousers back to order as he moved. He saw in dismay that the front of his trousers was soiled. He opened a magazine and put it in his lap.

Mari was curled up lazily on the love seat by the time the others entered, looking demure and innocent. Even Craig, glancing at her, could hardly believe that seconds before the girl had been squirming and moaning in the throes of paradise.

"You two enjoying yourselves?" Jackie asked as he accompanied Aunt Lily and Aunt Nasturtia into the room.

"Just waiting quietly for the rest of you," Craig explained innocently. "Thought I'd read while I was waiting."

Jackie made no comment, and Aunt Lily looked away, but Aunt Nasturtia was never one to display tact.

"How can you be reading?" she asked innocently. "Your magazine's upside down."

* * * * * * *

Although Jackie found Craig's embarrassment amusing, he could hardly criticize Craig for what had obviously taken place. After all, Jackie often used sex as a tool in his work, and regarded the pleasures derived therein as a natural reward for his efforts. In fact, he had used just such a modus operandi only a few minutes before, with amazingly good results.

It began with his visit to Mr. Bigelow, the last of the Bigelows on their list. Thus far all of the visits had been unsuccessful, and he had not entered the waiting room of the office marked A. Bigelow with any great hope.

Things began looking better, however, the moment he saw the handsome young man behind the desk there. Much more hospitable, he thought with approval, than the usual gum-chewing female.

"Is Mr. Bigelow in?" Jackie asked, allowing his eyes to make a round trip tour of the dark-haired stranger— via the scenic route. And a very scenic route it was, too. He was probably Greek, dark and romantic looking. He was short, not more than 5 feet 8 inches, and built rather stockily, with powerful, thick legs and wide hips, a thick waist and chest, and what was described as a bull neck. Definitely an armful, Jackie concluded with a wistful sigh.

"What do you do?" the handsome youth asked.

It seemed rather a direct approach, but Jackie was about to answer in detail when he realized that the young man might not be cruising. "Do?" he asked, playing it safe.

"What kind of act do you have? You are a performer, aren't you? Most of Mr. Bigelow's callers are, in any case."

So that was it—Mr. Bigelow's door had said nothing more than REPRESENTATION AND MANAGEMENT. He should have realized that smacked of an entrepreneur of some sort or another. And here was his golden opportunity to really check out Mr. Bigelow.

"Dancer," he said aloud, giving his best toothpaste-commercial smile. "Ballroom, ballet, tap, underwater —you name it, I dance it."

The Greek seemed amused, although slightly doubtful. "Mr. Bigelow is out just now. If you'd like to fill out one of these forms, I'll see that he gets it."

"But aren't you even going to let me audition for you? I'm really quite good. You've never danced until you've tripped about with me." Aside from wanting to get his hands on all that lovely Mediterranean flesh, Jackie had a hunch it might be worth his while to become friendly with this one. He might need someone to encourage Mr. Bigelow's interest in him.

The dark-haired one stood up and looked Jackie up and down slowly, as though making up his mind. Then, with another grin, he walked to a turntable built into one of the shelves and thumbed through a few records.

"Do you waltz?" he asked.

"Viennese?"

"Russian."

"Of course." Jackie counted out the beat as the music began, scratchy and a little off pitch, but a good record nonetheless. He opened his arms, and the Greek came into them. For a second Jackie had his doubts as to who was going to do what, but the Greek made it plain he was going to lead, and Jackie followed happily. This way he didn't have to worry about steering or watching the road, he had his hands free to play with the gadgets... although gadget seemed less appropriate than weapon. He was beginning to understand the symbolism of all those columns they had used in their architecture.

The record ended and the Greek went back to the phonograph. "How about a tango?" Jackie suggested. It was his turn to make a challenge.

"French?" That was the common one, and the easier of the choices.

"Argentine," Jackie said instead.

The Greek was surprised, but he didn't hesitate. The music began, and a minute later he was back, leading Jackie off at once into a sultry, torrid dance routine that had Jackie's blood boiling.

"Are you as good horizontally?" Jackie asked as his partner bent him far back and down, until his head almost touched the floor.

For an answer, his companion danced him silently across the office, circling the reception desk. With one flick of his wrist he deftly opened the door that led into the inner office. Jackie followed happily as he was piloted inside; the door closed after them. They were promenading in the direction of the huge divan against one wall. Unless he was sadly mistaken, he was about to have a lesson in "The Greek Style."

Short though his partner might have been, he was plenty strong, and he was still "leading." He lowered Jackie easily to the divan, kneeling over him. Instinctively Jackie lifted his face to kiss his partner. The kiss was neatly avoided, although the dark-haired youth was busy baring Jackie from the waist down.

Jackie remembered then his last experience with any of this one's countrymen. When it came to boys, they were game for sex any way but sideways. But they didn't go for any of that queer stuff like kissing! Oh, well, he thought philosophically, better half a loaf than none at all. Which was an appropriate thought, for at that moment his loaves were being treated to an ardent and pointed attention.

His friend was like a bull in more ways than one. In typical Mediterranean fashion, he was anything but gentle in his approach, a lusty, carved-marble battering ram that went straight for its destination, without any fooling around. Jackie felt the wind knocked out of his body as he was shoved back against the divan forcefully, his legs held high and wide apart in the Greek's brawny arms.

Yet despite the ferocity of his brutal attack, he had other ways of showing concern and affection. All the while his throbbing attention was threatening to split Jackie asunder, his big hands were fondling and stroking Jackie tenderly, and he had begun to whisper sweet nothings that, remembered afterward, would sound downright silly, but for the moment were so romantic and heartwarming that they all but made one forget what was happening out back.

The room spun crazily as Jackie surrendered himself to the sweet agony of the experience. Rarely had he ever felt so fulfilled, or been so thrilled. There was nothing halfway about his partner, or his technique. It was a complete taking, that demanded an equal giving.

The Greek had pushed Jackie's shirt up, and as his ardor grew into a raging fire, he bent closer, biting at the small, dusky nipples on Jackie's chest. Jackie threw his head back in delirious pleasure. He felt the surging finish approaching, groaned as the caresses became even more thorough and then, in an ultimate achievement, accepted the homage of his convulsive lover.

Jackie's success was complete. Not only did he feel utterly sated, but he had won himself a job as well.

"I'll see to it that you get some work," the Greek,

who had finally introduced himself as Nick, said afterward. "There's a special show on for Friday night. I'll see that you're in it."

Jackie's pulse quickened. Friday night was the scheduled time for the assassination referred to in the note. Was there a connection?

"Don't worry, he will do as I suggest," Nick answered with a grin. "I can be very persuasive."

Jackie grinned too. One could hardly blame Mr. Bigelow for being henpecked. It would be pretty difficult not to do as Nick suggested.

CHAPTER NINE

CRAIG LISTENED TO JACKIE'S story with interest. Jackie had omitted the details of his "friendship" with Nick, and had gone directly to the business of the upcoming special show. "I think it might be a lead," he said finally.

Craig shook his head grimly. "More so than you think. It could be merely a coincidence, but there is a benefit show being staged Friday night, for Viet Nam war orphans. I'd forgotten about it until now."

"Do you think it ties in with the assassination?"

"It very well might. There will be some important people there. As a matter of fact, the guest of honor will be my boss, the head of the C.I.A."

"Duval himself?" Jackie was astonished.

"He'll be in a special box. If they were planning to assassinate him, they couldn't pick a better opportunity."

"We could warn him right now...." Jackie paused thoughtfully. "But would he believe us? It's a farfetched scheme. And even if he did take our word for it, we'd take a chance on letting the Butterfly agents get away."

"We're taking a chance either way. If we let them go ahead with their plan, and then fail to stop them when the time comes, we'll both feel pretty rotten."

"I'm confident we won't fail," Jackie assured him. "But I'll leave the decision to you. On one hand, you've a chance to score a real coup against Butterfly. On the other, you're gambling with your entire career."

He knew the answer even before Craig spoke. "Go ahead and take that job with the show. And keep your eyes and ears wide open."

Jackie was relieved by the decision. He had been eager to get to work on the case. Each difficulty was to him merely another challenge, an obstacle to be surmounted through the use of his wits. Failure was a possibility he never allowed himself to consider.

"How are you at heart-to-heart talks?" Craig asked unexpectedly.

"Best shoulder in the world," Jackie answered. For the first time he realized that Craig seemed strangely preoccupied.

Craig also seemed embarrassed, as though he was forcing himself to explain. "You know about Mari and me?" he began, noting Jackie's quick nod. "Well, it was just a matter of being horny—at least, that's what I thought at the moment. Now I'm not so sure that I didn't have another motive, which I just wouldn't admit to myself."

"Such as?"

Craig was becoming increasingly embarrassed. "Well, I've never been around any...you know, *gay* fellows before. And if someone had said to me that someday I'd be curious about...well, how it was to do it with a guy...I'd have laughed at him. Now, all of a sudden, something crazy has happened. Believe me, I never thought I'd actually feel attracted to a fellow, no matter how special he was."

"And you are?" Jackie was amazed. He had not realized that Craig felt that way about him.

"I'm not sure. I still haven't made up my mind."

"Well, do me one little old favor," Jackie said with a pleased grin. "When you decide, just make sure I'm the first to know."

Craig seemed grateful that Jackie was taking all this in stride, without any I-told-you-so remarks. "I promise," he said quietly.

Jackie had been instructed to report to a downtown theater for a rehearsal of the show. When he arrived, an acrobatic act was being rehearsed on the stage. Nick saw him and came to greet him, accompanied by an auntie-ish individual who turned out to be Mr. Bigelow.

"Nick tells me your movements are quite phenomenal," Mr. Bigelow remarked. For the life of him, Jackie couldn't tell whether the man was referring to dancing or sex. Nick was grinning from behind Mr. Bigelow, obviously enjoying Jackie's uncertainty.

"They'll never be as good as Nick's," Jackie answered finally, pleased to see the grin disappear from Nick's face as Mr. Bigelow gave him a quick frown.

He took his place off stage and waited for his turn on stage to come up. As he waited and watched, he saw Mr. Bigelow and Nick disappear into an office backstage. Glancing about to be certain no one was watching him, Jackie followed them.

"It's all set," Mr. Bigelow was saying as Jackie paused outside the door, straining to hear the conversation. "The performers will leave here in the limousine, but Andre will have been replaced by a different driver. That way, we're in the clear. The driver will kidnap them and take them to that empty farmhouse outside the city. In the meantime, the other troupe, in an identical limousine, will take their place at the theater. You know the rest."

Jackie tensed with excitement. So this was it—the show was to be the opportunity for the assassination, and he now knew how it was going to be arranged. Now, if he could only learn just when during the show, and how....

To his dismay, one of the two had flicked on a radio inside, drowning out the sound of their voices. Jackie remained where he was, straining, but he could near nothing over the jazz music playing. He glanced around again. At the moment, no one was near. He bent and looked through the keyhole.

He understood why they had suddenly wanted to cut off any sounds from inside. They had finished with the other business, and were now busy with a different kind of business, one that was attached to the lower part of Nick's husky torso.

The handsome Greek's trousers had been pushed down about his ankles, leaving him naked from waist to feet. His hair-shaded legs were spread wide apart, his hands on his thrust-forward hips. And Mr. Bigelow was hungrily kissing the awesome sight that intruded in front of him.

Jackie tingled with excitement as he saw the scene. Part of the excitement came from the memory of Nick's body, and the wish that he could be in Bigelow's place; but there was more than that. As Bigelow's head pulled back, away from Nick's abdomen, Nick's flesh was exposed in full glory. Thanks to their positions, Jackie had not really gotten a look the other time, although he had certainly wanted to. Now, however, even at this distance he could easily make out the mark on it, the tattoo.

It was unmistakably the Butterfly design. He had assumed Nick was only a hustler, a current trick of Bigelow's. Now he realized that Nick was a member of

Butterfly, and high up in the hierarchy. The tattoo was worn only by those in the upper echelons.

There was a sound nearby, and Jackie sprang to his feet. Someone had come off the stage, and Jackie moved away from the office before he could be noticed. He wasn't going to learn any more just now. But at least he knew enough to begin making a few plans of his own.

* * * * * * *

"Do you think it will work?" Craig remained unconvinced, although the others were in enthusiastic accord.

"I don't see why it shouldn't," Aunt Lily said bluntly. "It sounds foolproof to me."

"Well, not exactly foolproof." Jackie was quick to ward off any arguments. "But if everyone does his part properly, we should make it work. Now, let's go over it once again."

Everyone became quite serious, listening silently and attentively as Jackie explained the scheme for the fourth time.

"They're planning on kidnapping the real troupe," he said. "Of course, I'll be along with them. My job will be to get rid of their driver, and deliver the original performers to the theater instead of the substitute troupe."

He paused to look around and assure himself that each of them was with him so far. "All right. Now, in the meantime, Craig will be with his boss—that's our insurance policy, just in case everything else fails."

"I'd still rather be doing something more active," Craig protested.

"And we could use you. But we need you where you'll be. We have to know that, no matter what else happens, you won't fail in protecting your boss."

Craig grunted. "I guess you're right," he admitted grudgingly.

"That means," Jackie went on, "that we have to get rid of the other troupe they've prepared, the phony performers. Aunt Nasturtia, that's where you and Mari come in. You must understand, it's dangerous. You are to do nothing directly. All we want is for you to delay them. Get lost, or whatever is necessary, to allow me to get the others there first. If the other performers are already on stage when they arrive, there won't be much they can do. And anyway, by that time I'll be there waiting for them."

"And we'll be there too," Aunt Lily said proudly.

"That's right. You, Honey, and Gladiola will be at the theater, as reserve troops. If there's any delay in my arrival, Honey, you'll have to save the day by going on stage and pretending to be the opening act of the show."

"Don't worry," Honey assured him. "They'll think they're listening to Von Clabborn."

It was, Jackie decided, a simple enough plot. The only likelihood of failure was in Aunt Nasturtia's hands. And he had an idea for minimizing that.

He had already learned that the phony troupe would be leaving from Bigelow's office, and he had seen the Cadillac limousine that he suspected would be used to deliver them to the theater. It was not difficult to find an identical limousine, and with a little work, it was converted into a fine booby trap.

"Now," he said, showing the results to Aunt Nasturtia. "If anything goes wrong—if there's any trouble from the people you're driving—you have only to press this switch, and the rear of the car will immediately be filled with knockout gas. It's harmless, but it will put them to sleep in seconds."

"What if they jump out of the car?"

"Impossible. This second switch electrically locks all the doors. They can't get out until you let them out from the front. And the window between the driver's compartment and the rear is bulletproof. Just be certain that it's up at all times."

"Now let me see," Aunt Nasturtia said, mentally reviewing all that she had been told. "How am I going to get them in the car?"

"That's Mari's part," Jackie explained again. "They're expecting a limousine to pull up at the rear door for them. But when the right one arrives, Mari will approach the driver and persuade him to take her to the other side of the parking lot. As soon as they pull away, you're to pull up to the door and honk the horn for the performers. If anyone asks about your impatience, you'll show them your watch, which will be ten minutes fast, and explain that they're late."

"Then all I do is drive around?" Nasturtia said.

"Until eight forty-five. By that time, I should be there. But you'll hear the signal. They're broadcasting the entire show, and the opening act, by luck, is a pianist. He'll play the 'Bolero.' When you hear that, you'll know it's safe to bring them to the theater."

It was, then, a simple enough plot—assuming, of course, that everything went as planned.

CHAPTER TEN

AS THE TIME OF the special benefit show drew nearer, Jackie grew uneasy. Was he only being silly, or was his intuition right in warning him of problems? Whichever it was, however, he kept such thoughts to himself, maintaining a show of cheerful confidence so far as the others were concerned, Craig particularly.

Craig remained unhappy over the fact that he would not be in the action at all, but he accepted Jackie's judgment on the matter. It was essential to have the added insurance—they could not afford to fail in protecting Duval.

Time came at last for Jackie to depart for the practice theater, where the car would pick up the performers and allegedly deliver them to the plush Herald theater, where the show was taking place. Jackie went over the plans with the others one last time. Gladiola, Honey, and Lily were to go directly to the Herald theater, and be prepared to do whatever might prove necessary to assist the others. Craig, of course, would be meeting his superior, and would accompany him. And Mari and Aunt Nasturtia were to follow Jackie to the practice theater, where they would arrange their kidnapping feat.

At last, convinced that he had done all he could do, Jackie packed a bag with the costume he would wear and departed in a cab for Bigelow's theater.

The other performers were already there, busily dressing or making-up. It had been planned that the performers would ready themselves here, prior to being driven to the special show. Jackie joined the various male entertainers in the dressing room and quickly changed into the tights and jersey that would be his costume for the evening.

"I don't think I've ever seen you perform before," one of the entertainers addressed him as Jackie applied his make-up. "Have you worked in this area much?"

"Not at all," Jackie answered truthfully, careful not to make a statement that would trip him up. "I've been working on the West Coast, and just came into town recently."

"Well, good luck," the man said. He was, Jackie knew from rehearsals, a singer, and something of a loner. He seemed, from time to time, to be cruising, but it was hard to say for certain. At another time, Jackie would probably have made it a point to determine whether he was or not. At the present, however, he had other things on his mind.

He would like to have known just where the other performers were, the ones who would be substituted for this group. He knew they were somewhere in the same theater, for the plans called for them to be picked up from Bigelow's office. But he did not dare risk looking around for them. He could only hope, as the time came for departure, that everything would go as planned.

The limousine arrived for him and his fellow performers right on schedule. There were only seven of them—the pianist, a vocal group, and an acrobatic troupe, plus himself. Jackie's plans to thwart this kidnapping depended upon his being able to get to the driver. As they climbed into the limousine, Jackie boldly climbed into the front with the chauffeur.

"Sorry, you'll have to sit in the back," the driver told him in a surly voice.

Jackie giggled and flipped a wrist. "Don't be such a goose. It's hot, and it's too crowded back there for all of us. Besides, I won't grope you, if that's what you're afraid of." Without waiting for the driver to have a change of heart, he slammed the door and settled back in the seat.

His bluff worked. The driver seemed unhappy over the situation, but he chose not to argue it further. Jackie remained in the front as the car moved away from the theater.

They weren't attempting to be subtle. The car was

moving in the exact opposite direction from the one it should have been taking. From the corner of his eye, Jackie could see some of the others exchanging glances. The glass had been closed between the front and rear compartments, and when the pianist knocked on the glass, the driver ignored the summons altogether.

"Aren't we going the wrong way?" Jackie asked innocently. He wanted to play it dumb until it was safe to take over control of the car. In his pocket, however, his fingers curled around the handle of a jeweled derringer, the gun he always carried when he was working on a case. It was a single shot affair, and not good for anything beyond a short distance.

It was all that he usually needed, however, and safer for his purposes than the more lethal weapons available. For one thing, he had no special license to kill; his training, in fact, had carefully prepared him to avoid killing except as a necessity, in self-defense.

They turned unexpectedly and sharply into a darkened alley. Another quick turn, while the passengers in the rear sat forward in alarm, and they were in a dark and deserted parking area behind some warehouses. Jackie had not counted on this, but as he saw the moving van that pulled into the lot from another alley, he realized that they were about to be transferred to the other vehicle. He had planned on their being kept in this car, but he could see now that, from their kidnapers' standpoint, a moving van would be safer.

The limousine had stopped. Jackie's hand tightened on the derringer as the chauffeur pulled a gun, an ominous-looking Luger.

"Everybody out," he said, waving the gun menacingly. "And into the van."

Genuinely frightened, the others obeyed, scrambling out of the limousine. Jackie got out on his own side, waiting for a chance. The driver circled the car, motioning them toward the van. Jackie saw the beady eyes look aside, checking for witnesses. It was his chance. He dropped behind a fender, and fired. His aim was perfect. The chauffeur yelped and dropped the gun as the bullet tore through his hand. With lightning speed, Jackie was in front of him, and had the Luger.

"Now then," he said, brandishing the weapon. "What about your friends in the van—are they armed?"

"They aren't," a voice said behind him. "But I am."

Jackie felt a threatening poke at his spine. He didn't have to ask—he knew the feel of a gun in his back. Cursing himself silently, he dropped the Luger to the ground.

"That's better," the singer said. "Now, you'll kindly join the others at the moving van."

"You won't get away with this," Jackie told him as he walked obediently toward the moving van.

"We'll see," the other said. "I'm just glad we decided

to include me in the group, just in case. Nick had a hunch someone might have gotten wise."

"Is Nick the boss?" Jackie asked, his mind working rapidly as usual. Eventually he would make an escape, and he might as well collect all the information possible.

"Right you are," his companion answered. They had reached the van. The others, frightened and bewildered by the fast exchange of advantages, were already huddled inside. Jackie was prodded with the gun, and he climbed reluctantly inside. There was no opportunity to try for the gun. No sooner was he inside the van, than the door was slammed quickly shut and bolted noisily in place. He shoved against it at once, but it was sealed tightly. Like it or not, they were prisoners inside the truck.

* * * * * * *

Aunt Nasturtia pulled the car into the darkened edge of the parking lot, switching off the engine quickly. The big Cadillac was quite a change from the older model car which they had at the house, and which she was accustomed to driving. Still, things were going smoothly.

"You're on," she said to Mari, beside her in the front seat.

Mari checked herself in her compact mirror, gave the bodice of her dress a final downward tug, and opened the car door. "Here's hoping he likes blondes," she said. With a grin and a wave, she was gone.

Jackie had coached her carefully about how she was to play the scene. The driver of the other limousine must think she was from the theater, so that he would be less suspicious. For that, she had to get inside the theater, and emerge from there.

She found the side door that Jackie had described, and as he had assured her, it was unlocked. She slipped inside and moved lightly down the hall, following his directions. A turn, then another, and she was approaching the rear door, the one at which she should find the waiting limousine.

It was there, just as planned. She groaned inwardly as she saw the driver—one of those shifty, greasy types that she didn't really go for. Oh well, she thought philosophically, with his pants down that wouldn't matter—anyway, she was being patriotic. That was the one thing she liked about this kind of work. You got to carry on a lot, and no one could say you were being immoral—it was your duty, after all.

She approached the open window on the driver's side of the car. He looked up and leered as she approached, swinging her wide hips seductively. Her breasts bounced and jiggled freely within the loose confines of the dress.

"Got a match?" she asked, leaning against the side

of the car. Her breasts swayed in the window opening, practically grazing his nose. His eyes were as wide as saucers.

"Sure," he managed to sputter, gulping loudly. She half expected him to lean out and bite one of the nipples just to see if they were real.

"Lonesome?" she asked when he had lit the cigarette for her with trembling hands.

"I'm waiting for some people," he said in a voice that told her he wasn't going to put up much resistance. With that face, she thought to herself, he probably didn't get too many propositions.

"Doesn't look like they're here yet. As long as you're just killing time, wouldn't you rather kill it together?"

He was having a real battle with himself, she could see that. His thighs were yelling for him to take her up on the offer; his fear of whoever he worked for was telling him to stay where he was.

"Look," she said, fluttering her eyelashes. "We could pull just over there." She pointed to the other end of the dark parking lot, opposite the place where Nasturtia was parked. "We can see your friends when they come out, all right?"

"All right," he finally agreed, his head bobbing. Mari came around the car and slid inside, moving all the way across the seat to press against him. He was scarcely able to start up the car and pull into the parking lot.

When they were parked, Mari saw to it that he was turned away from the theater's exit. She didn't want him to see what was going on there. That meant, of course, keeping him occupied. She kissed him hotly, rubbing her big breasts against his chest. One shaking hand slipped nervously under her skirt. She pushed her legs apart boldly, inviting him to explore, and dropped her own hand to his legs.

What she found was a pleasant surprise—this wasn't going to be such a disappointing bit after all. She was only sorry she didn't have a sack to put over his head, in which case it could be a really glorious occasion. As it was, however, she was busy watching the back window. She saw Aunt Nasturtia pull up to the door, and a few minutes later the phony performers had trouped out of the theater and were in the car. Mari smiled with relief as she saw Aunt Nasturtia drive away with her guests.

Work was over, now she could concentrate on playing. Her companion had been trying hard to get her arranged on the seat. She helped him accomplish the feat now, closing her eyes. He wasn't much to look at, but he was wonderful to feel—and she was feeling plenty.

CHAPTER ELEVEN

"WHAT'S HAPPENING?" The voice, Jackie guessed in the darkness, belonged to one of the acrobats.

"To put it very simply, we're being kidnapped." Jackie slammed his fist into the palm of his other hand as the truck started up, moving slowly at first as they went down the alley, and then gathering speed as they apparently reached the street.

"But why?" This was a feminine voice, belonging to one of the singing group.

"It's a little hard to explain," Jackie answered. He was thinking frantically. It had been his assumption that they would only be held, or even driven around, until the assassination had been completed at the theater. The fact that more elaborate plans had been made must mean that they weren't any of them intended to live to tell what had happened. Some accident would happen, something that would effectively destroy this truck, and them with it. And for the moment, he was at a loss how he could prevent it.

He thought of Aunt Nasturtia, who even now would be driving off with her carful of bogus entertainers. She was only expecting to delay them briefly—but unless he could escape from the interior of this fast moving truck, there would be no performers to start the show.

Moving carefully in the dark, he reached inside his mouth with one hand. At the back of his mouth, one wisdom tooth came loose in answer to his tugging. It was a fake, a clever counterfeit of a tooth that was in actuality a miniature bomb, a capsule of high-powered explosives that escaped detection in the event of a search, and gave him an ace in the hole.

The explosive would be sufficient to blow open the door of the van, of that he was certain. But the fallacy in that plan was apparent. The explosion would be certain to harm the people inside the van as well.

"What's going to happen to us?" Someone asked in the darkness.

"Nothing, if I can help it," Jackie assured him. "But to do that, I've got to get out of here somehow. Does anyone have a match?"

"I've got a lighter," the pianist suggested. "But where in blazes are you?"

"Follow my voice," Jackie instructed, "and keep talking. I'll try to find you too."

He moved slowly, balancing himself to the sway of

the truck, following the sound of the pianist's voice. He reached out, and found himself with a handful of something that, despite the fabric covering it, was obviously masculine.

"I think you found me," the pianist said with a chuckle. He did not, Jackie noticed, move away from the hand that was still holding him gently.

"Nice to meet you," Jackie said into the darkness. He gave the tensing flesh a gentle squeeze. It would be pleasant...but there was work to be done, he reminded himself with a sigh, and took his hand away, feeling for the lighter instead.

He answered the pianist's smile in the flickering light from the lighter before he devoted his attention to the interior of the van.

"Just as I thought," he said aloud. "A hatch in the top."

The others looked up too, and saw the square opening in the roof of the van, covered with a trapdoor type covering.

"Someone will have to boost me up there," Jackie said, flicking out the lighter as it began to grow too warm to hold.

"That's right down our alley," one of the acrobats said. He moved toward where Jackie was standing. "Give me your hand."

Jackie reached for and found the hand of the acrobat.

The other tumbler joined them, and the two of them managed easily to lift the agent upward.

It was no easy task. The truck was moving rapidly now, and turning frequently, following some rambling route. It took precision balance on the part of the two men to hold him up. Jackie reached the door above and pushed. It refused to budge.

"Maybe if one of us tried," the one fellow below suggested.

"No, help me get my shoe off," Jackie said instead. They managed to remove his shoe and hand it up to him. Jackie twisted the heel and it gave to reveal a concealed compartment. Inside was a small metal bar, designed to be used as a lever. Handing his shoe back down, he fitted the bar into the hatch and pried. It yielded, very slowly at first and then, with a groan of rusty hinges, it swung upward. The wind caught it and helped to fling it all the way back.

"That's it. Hang on to me until I get a good grip up here." With the two men below supporting him, Jackie managed to lift himself half out of the opening. He signaled to them to let go.

"I don't know what will happen," he warned them as he hung suspended. "Get down on the floor and cover your heads with your arms, just in case there's a crash. I'll do what I can to prevent it."

With his miniature bomb in his hand, he pulled

himself up and onto the top of the truck. They were moving out of the city now, on some back street that he didn't recognize. As he crouched on the domed top of the truck, a shot rang out, and a bullet ricocheted off the metal near him.

He looked behind. The Cadillac limousine was following them, and one of the men in the car had spotted him. Keeping as low as possible, Jackie inched toward the front of the truck. He had to get inside the cab, and somehow gain control of the truck.

Behind him, the Cadillac was pulling closer, the gunman trying to get a better aim at him. And they were succeeding. The bullets were whizzing ever closer. Jackie held the explosive capsule in his hand. He could fling it now, and put the Cadillac out of commission—but that would leave him virtually weaponless. He might need the fake tooth when he got inside the cab of the truck.

He decided to bide his time. Keeping as low as he possibly could, he crept forward. The truck was moving fast, too fast for his comfort. One false move and he would be thrown free.

He neared the cab of the truck—the going was getting trickier. Now he would have to go over the side and reach the door. Even then, he would have to prevent himself from being knocked off the running board by the driver.

He took a firm hold on a piece of molding and began to lower himself over the side. Behind them, the men in the Cadillac had spotted him again and guessed his maneuver. They were pulling out to come alongside the truck. He would be a sitting duck for them.

He watched as the big car nosed into the left lane and shot forward, racing toward him. With one hand, Jackie twisted the capsule, setting the detonator, and hurled it at the windshield of the car.

It went off with a powerful noise and a cloud of smoke. The windshield went, and took with it, from what he could see, a good portion of the driver's face. The Cadillac careened crazily across the road and then back. Jackie thought for a moment that it would run right into him, but it didn't. Instead, it sideswiped the cab of the truck and then bounced across the ditch where it came to a stop at last.

The collision had been too slight to do much damage to the truck, but it was enough to cause the driver to come to a sudden stop. Jackie dropped lightly to the ground as the door opened and the driver of the truck leaped out. He had only half turned before Jackie hit him, shooting forward like a rocket. They went down together, hitting the concrete with a thud.

Jackie had rolled with the man as they fell, and the driver landed beneath him. The landing was enough to stun him, and Jackie put him soundly to sleep with a fist in the jaw.

There was a shot behind him, and sparks flew up from the spot where the bullet struck the roadway. Jackie fell flat, turning as he dropped. The other man from the truck was firing from inside.

The driver's gun lay inches away. Jackie stretched, reaching it at last with his fingers. He crawled behind the scant bulk of the driver's body, using the man for a shield.

He couldn't afford to waste bullets on bad shots. He waited, watching intently for that vital second when the man in the truck raised his head to aim again. Jackie fired once, and the man fell against the window sill.

Jackie took only a second to stick his head inside the truck and tell the others that everything was all right now, and that they were on their way back to town. Then, dragging the two men from the truck to the side of the road, he climbed behind the wheel of the truck and turned it carefully around, heading at top speed back into the city.

* * * * * * *

Nasturtia drove away from the theater with a triumphant grin on her face. Everything was going exactly as planned. Now she had only to stall until the coast was clear. She flicked on the radio and tuned it to the station that would be carrying the program.

It was now about eight-fifteen. The program was scheduled to begin at eight-thirty. Jackie had assured her that by eight-forty-five he would be there, and the real performers would be beginning the program. With Ravel's "Bolero," he had said.

She headed west, making her way surely but subtly away from the theater where they were to do the show. If only her passengers did not suspect anything, or notice the route they were taking.

By eight thirty, she had managed to circle about the city and put them some considerable distance from the theater. But her passengers suddenly noticed the time. One of them tapped angrily on the glass separating the two compartments and pointed to his watch.

Nasturtia, her gray hair concealed by the chauffeur's cap, nodded her head, and proceeded to take yet another wrong turn. This one, however, was recognized for what it was. The man in the back seat drew a gun and waved it at her.

Aunt Nasturtia decided to use the emergency equipment, but which of those switches did what? Jackie had explained it all to her so patiently, and now it had all fled from her memory. With a silent prayer, she flipped one of the switches. There was a click as the rear doors were unlocked. Without thinking to turn the switch back, she tried another. This time the bulletproof glass that protected her from her passengers began to glide downward. In dismay, she tried the last. The gas began pouring into the car with a loud hiss. Regrettably, it did not confine itself to the back seat, but billowed into the front through the opened glass.

Nasturtia rolled her eyes, trying to get a window open. In the back, the passengers had already managed to open windows and were hanging outside, gulping in fresh air.

She found the buttons that raised and lowered the windows. With the first one, she managed to choke one of the passengers in the rear who had been hanging his head outside the car. He was too slow to escape the ascent of the window, and was pinned by the neck.

Nasturtia made a groggy attempt at another button, but she was too sleepy to make it. The car reeled crazily and veered across the street, coming finally to a violent stop against a utility pole.

Of all the people in the car, only Nasturtia and the man whose head was caught in the window were unconscious. The others were quite conscious enough to start back for the theater.

CHAPTER TWELVE

"ANYTHING YET?" HONEY came back to where Gladiola was standing backstage at the theater. Craig had managed to get the three of them inside as theater personnel. Gladiola, as agreed, was watching as look-out man.

"Not a thing," she declared wearily, rolling her eyes. It was already well after eight-thirty. Outside the audience was growing restless and impatient. People were milling about backstage, watching anxiously for some sign of the performers. Mr. Bigelow, whom Honey recognized from the pictures Jackie had shown him, was there, with a handsome young Greek man. The handsome Greek seemed especially nervous over the delay. But then, Honey reflected, he had every reason to be.

"I think you'd better prepare to put the emergency plan into operation," Aunt Lily suggested. "According to schedule, Jackie should have been here by now. We can't delay much longer."

The emergency plan called for Honey to begin the

show. It was a bold move—he would have to walk on stage right past the managers and other personnel, take his seat at the piano, and start as though he belonged there. They were gambling on the probability that no one would dare run on stage and drag him away in front of the entire audience.

They had already managed discreetly to pick out a dressing room that was empty, and there they had hidden clothing for the emergency plan. Honey disappeared inside and emerged a few minutes later in tails.

His heart was pounding loudly as he shouldered his way through the crowd backstage. No one paid him any attention—they were all too preoccupied with the delay to notice him until he had pushed past the stage manager. Then, with heads turning sharply in his direction, he straightened his jacket and marched brazenly onstage.

The audience, scarcely likely to know that he was not the intended performer, greeted him with applause, although his tardiness dampened their enthusiasm somewhat.

Honey accepted the applause with a curt little bow and then seated himself at the piano. The program called for the "Bolero"—which he did not know. In fact, he still knew nothing but the first movement from the "Moonlight Sonata." And with that he began the show.

He played with a lack of ability and talent unique in the annals of music, unique even in his own experience. Only by accident did he manage to play any correct notes.

The audience sat as though stunned, as indeed they might well have been. There was no applause when he finished the first movement. He knew only that movement, and so had no choice but to begin again, the number of mistakes increasing the second time through.

With one eye he watched the offstage area. People were glowering and motioning, even shaking their fists at him. So far, however, no one had come after him—nor was there any signal from Aunt Lily or Gladiola that Jackie had arrived. Determined to stay where he was until Jackie came to take over, Honey played valiantly on.

Backstage, pandemonium reigned. Everyone was cursing everyone else in barely suppressed voices. Aunt Lily went to stand near Gladiola, so that both would be close to the exit. As luck would have it, however, a curtain concealed them from Mr. Bigelow when they heard him discussing them with a stagehand.

"We'll get him off that stage if we have to shoot him first. And find those two women he was talking to. Lock them up in the basement till this is all over."

The two women exchanged frightened glances.

Things were getting rapidly out of hand, and they could no longer afford to wait here for Jackie. It was time to take cover.

"Come on," Lily said, dragging Gladiola with her. They reached the dressing room Honey had used and darted inside, leaning anxiously against the door.

"It'll be a matter of minutes before they look for us here," Lily said, looking about the small room. "The best thing for us to do is find disguises of some sort. There must be costumes here."

Gladiola checked the closet, which was virtually bare. She spotted a large trunk and lifted the lid.

"Hot dog," she exclaimed, holding up a garment. "A whole trunk of costumes."

"We're in luck." Aunt Lily left the door and came to the trunk, rummaging through the clothes. "Find something, anything, and get it on fast. We've got to get out of here and disappear into the crowd outside."

Regrettably, the costumes in the trunk were not the disappearing type. Aunt Lily was finally able to find a costume from "Carmen" that fit her. With the addition of a lace shawl over her gray hair, she looked not unlike one of those notorious cigarette ladies.

"It's hardly inconspicuous, but it will have to do," she said, smoothing out a paper rose at her waist. "But what about you?"

"They ain't none of this going to fit my fat body,"

Gladiola said morosely.

"They must have something here," Lily insisted. She dug through the outfits again, and came up finally with a full length leotard, bright red. "Here, this stretches," she said, shoving the fabric into Gladiola's hands.

The material did indeed stretch. The result, however, was like nothing ever seen before. Gladiola's huge figure bulged in the most improbable places beneath the fiery red cloth.

Lily found a tutu, a pink, fluffy affair. The result was even worse, nor did the addition of ballet slippers and a blonde headpiece help.

"Lord, they'll shoot me and ask questions later," Gladiola said, examining her reflection in the mirror.

"It's the best we can do," Lily said philosophically. "Besides, they know that there are dancers in the show, but not what kind. With luck, they'll just think you're a ballerina."

Gladiola snorted her disbelief, but she followed close behind Aunt Lily as she opened the door and slipped out of the room.

"Best split up," Lily said in a whisper. "I'll circle around to the other side of the stage, you stay over this way. Keep your eyes peeled for Jackie. It's up to him now."

Gladiola positioned herself in the protective safety of a curtain. With an indolent sway of her hips, Lily made her way slowly through the crowds, acting for all the world as though she were in her realm.

She reached the opposite side of the backstage area without incident. On the stage, Honey had just begun the first movement of the "Moonlight Sonata" for the third time, to the growing annoyance of the audience, who were talking loudly now, voicing their protests.

Aunt Lily looked back over her shoulder, at precisely the wrong moment. Bigelow emerged from behind a flat and saw her. His eyes narrowed as he recognized her despite the disguise. She saw his hand move toward his jacket; she didn't have to be told that he had a gun there.

The stage hands were all busy watching Honey, trying frantically to get his attention. It was her only route of escape. Swallowing mightily, she stepped past them, and on to the stage.

Even Honey was startled by her unexpected appearance, enough so that he stopped playing. Lily flashed him a smile and hurried across the stage. She was about to exit from the opposite side, when she saw the stage-hand to whom Bigelow had spoken waiting for her.

There was nothing to do but remain where she was. She turned and curtsied in the direction of the audience. Then, stepping closer to the footlights, she cleared her throat and began to sing the only song she could remember in its entirety—"The Last Rose of

Summer"—in a cracked, off-pitch voice.

At the piano, a bewildered Honey was trying desperately to offer her assistance by striking keys that resembled slightly the notes she was singing. By the time she had managed the first verse, they were very nearly together.

Gladiola, however, chose to join them for the second verse. The choice was not so much hers as dictated by necessity, for she had been spotted by Bigelow's friend. She had seen the others safe on the stage, and it seemed only right that she should join them. With a loud whoop that was intended for a high C, she bounded onto the stage, arms flailing, toes pointed. Her impersonation of a ballerina was somewhat marred by her lack of grace, and her ludicrous appearance. All in all, the effect was rather that of a mad water buffalo, in tutu and tights, charging across the stage.

The spectacle was one the likes of which no one in the audience had seen before. Mercifully, from their standpoint, it was brief. Bigelow gave the order to drop the curtain. It came down swiftly, trapping Honey and Gladiola behind it, and leaving Lily in front. Lily looked behind her, assessed the situation promptly, and scrambled down over the footlights to the aisle. It was time to make an escape.

A stage hand appeared from the wings and bounded after her, in hot pursuit up the aisle, while the members of the audience watched in astonishment.

The man had almost caught up with her when Lily heard Craig Mathews' welcome voice. "Oh, no you don't," he said loudly.

Lily stopped and looked back in time to see Craig fell the man with one solid blow to the jaw. "You all right?" he asked, looking up at her.

"I think so," she panted, giving him a wan smile. She opened her mouth to explain to him that something had gone wrong, but the words froze in her throat. From backstage, they heard the sound of gunshots, loud and ominous.

Lily and Craig exchanged frightened glances. "Come on," he said, breaking the spell. He ran back down the aisle toward the stage, with Lily close behind him.

* * * * * * *

Gladiola was scarcely aware of the descending curtain; she was, in fact, rather enjoying her dance debut. She made one final leap, right into the arms of Bigelow himself. Amid squeals and yelps, the two of them fell to the floor together.

Honey made a dash for the wings. Nick had appeared on the scene as well, and he stepped in front of the piano virtuoso, gun drawn.

It was at that moment that Jackie appeared, gun in hand. He fired once, shooting the gun from Nick's hand. Nick turned and would have bolted, but another bullet lodged in his ankle, and he fell to the floor.

Bigelow was still on the floor, helpless beneath Gladiola's considerable weight. Bigelow's other henchman, the stage hand, hesitated only briefly before raising his hand.

Craig arrived seconds later, with Lily close at his heels. It took only minutes to clear everything up. Duval, the C.I.A. chief, was summoned from the audience, along with Miss Temple who, under the guise of going to powder her nose, was trying to escape. Duval was quickly apprised of the situation and, by the time the carload of bogus performers arrived, with Nasturtia as their prisoner, there were plenty of reinforcements on hand to help corral them.

It proved to be a highly successful venture. Nick, as it turned out, was the chief of operations for the entire American branch of Butterfly, and Bigelow was his right hand man. Never before had arrests been made of two individuals so high in the ranks of that organization, and Craig was promised a just reward for his efforts.

The show, finally, was able to go on, with the real performers making appearances. Apologies were made to the audience, and brief explanations, and Honey, Gladiola and Lily were all called to the stage to take bows. After the initial shock, the audience had found their show quite amusing after all.

"Well, we gambled, but it looks like we won," Jackie said to Craig as they watched the last of the show from the wings.

Craig, however, seemed to be a thousand miles away. After a silence, he finally said, "You know, that conversation we had before, about my being attracted to another male?"

"Do I?" Jackie asked with a grin. "Have you made up your mind yet?"

Craig nodded his head solemnly. "Yes, I know now that I'll never be happy until I try it, and I've decided to try it right away, tonight, before I chicken out."

Jackie's heart caught in his throat. There was no more delightful climax to a case than a bedroom tumble with a new playmate, particularly someone as handsome and—well, virginal as Craig.

"I think that's the nicest thing I've heard in months," he said, with tears of happiness in his eyes. Already he could envision Craig, in naked glory, in his arms. They wouldn't either of them get any sleep tonight.

Craig smiled faintly. He was too occupied with his thoughts to be even aware of what was going on around him.

"Hey, I'll need the address of your apartment," Jackie reminded him. He couldn't very well take Craig to Aunt Lily's, where he shared a room with Honey.

"What?" Craig asked dimly. "Oh, my apartment. Sure, I'll write it down." He wrote the address on a scrap of paper and handed it to Jackie. "There's always a key in the mailbox."

* * * * * * *

Jackie could hardly wait for the evening to pass. The thought of his night with Craig had him in a virtual state of hysteria by the time he finally dropped Aunt Lily and the other women off at the house. Honey had gone separately, explaining that he had plans for the evening. Not, Jackie had thought with pride, as nice as mine—but he hadn't said it aloud. He never liked to gloat over his triumphs.

He found Craig's apartment building without difficulty. He was even later than he had anticipated, but the delay had been justified. He had stopped on the way for cold champagne, and glasses.

It was not hard to find his way—Craig had left a light on for him in what he assumed was the bedroom. Walking on tiptoe, Jackie made his way to the open door and paused.

Craig's back was turned to him, naked and glowing in the soft light. His bottom was every bit as magnificent as Jackie had imagined it, a wide curvaceous temple of pleasure. It was bent now as Craig crouched over the bed, and it was moving slowly downward.

The descent was laborious but apparently pleasurable, judging from the soft moans of pleasure emitting from the bed.

In addition to Craig's bewitching derriere, Jackie was also afforded a view of Honey's quite excited and tense outline. A limited view, to be sure, because more than half of it had already been claimed by Craig. And Honey was moaning too as he explored those recently-virginal delights. Neither of them were even aware Jackie had entered the room.

After the initial shock, Jackie backed quietly out of the room and stood in the darkness of the living room. Well, Craig hadn't really said what male it was he had been attracted to. For a brief moment, Jackie felt cheated by this turn of events. Then, his good humor returned to him.

You can't win them all, he told himself philosophically. He left the champagne on the table for them, along with a piece of note paper on which he had simply written "Best Wishes" to the new couple. Then he tiptoed from the apartment and returned to the late night darkness outside the building.

Good humor or no good humor, however, the evening had proved to be a waste. It was too late now to make the rounds of the local night spots. There was nothing for him to do but make his way home alone to Aunt Lily's and an empty bed. It was a hell of a way to spend what he had decided was his last night in town.

While he was standing outside Craig's apartment building, a lone sailor came down the street, walking quickly to ward off the late night chill. He was in summer white's, the uniform fitted tightly to a young, faun-like body that moved with natural grace. Jackie automatically looked at him, glancing up and down. He smiled with pleasure at what he saw—pleasures enough for a thousand and one nights—or at least for one good one.

He lifted his face to find the sailor glancing in his direction as he passed. Jackie smiled and winked boldly. The sailor blushed crimson and went on by, but his pace slowed at once. By the time he reached the corner intersection, a few feet away, he was barely moving.

He looked back over his shoulder, shyly, hesitantly, and finally managed an uncertain smile. Jackie gave the curvy buttocks, molded by the clinging fabric of the white uniform, a happy glance. It was the equal of anything he had seen tonight. With that thought, he started off in the direction of the corner, and the waiting sailor.

ABOUT THE AUTHOR

VICTOR J. BANIS is the critically acclaimed author ("...a master storyteller"—*Publishers Weekly*) of more than 200 published novels and numerous shorter works in a career spanning nearly a half century. A longtime Californian, he lives and writes now in West Virginia's beautiful Blue Ridge region.

www.ingramcontent.com/pod-product-compliance
Lightning Source LLC
Chambersburg PA
CBHW050755250626
47155CB00005B/2078